ACCOLADES FOR *ARTSY-FARTSY*

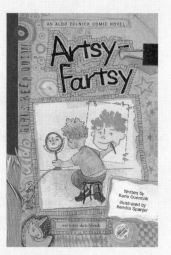

Artsy-Fartsy *is the first book in the alphabetical*
Aldo Zelnick comic novel series.

2009 Book of the Year Award bronze winner, juvenile fiction,
ForeWord Reviews

2009 Book of the Year Award finalist, graphic novel,
ForeWord Reviews

2010 Next Generation Indie Book Award finalist,
children's/juvenile fiction

2010 Colorado Book Award winner, juvenile fiction

2010 Mountains & Plains Independent Booksellers Association
award winner, children's chapter book

WHAT READERS ARE SAYING:

(kid comments are in Aldo's handwriting)

"It was the funniest book I have ever read. The illustrations are hilarious. It is better than Diary of a Wimpy Kid."

- Tavis

"We got *Artsy-Fartsy* last week and my son (who thinks he has better things to do than read) has not put it down since. He devoured the *Wimpy Kid* books but said he likes *Artsy-Fartsy* better because it's funnier. I like it better because it makes kids think. It's fun to hear giggles coming from the family room and my son is NOT watching TV."

- C. Maguire

"Greg Heffley and Ellie McDoodle, move over–Aldo Zelnick is here!"

— Mary Lee Hahn, teacher and readingyear.blogspot blogger

"I received Artsy-Fartsy *yesterday in the school mail. I am the media specialist at an elementary school. This book is fabulous, and I want to read it to ALL my classes! I love the vocabulary, humor, everything! Wonderful job!"*

- Sandy Schierman

"I REALLY LIKED YOUR ARTSY-FARTSY BOOK. I WOULD PUT IT ON MY TOP 10 LIST."

- Zach

"The other night I caught my 8-year-old twins giggling on the living room couch as they took turns reading *Artsy-Fartsy* aloud to each other. Then one morning I found it on their nightstand with a headlamp resting on the cover from the previous night's under-cover reading. That's a true badge of honor in this house. You hit this one out of the park."

- Becky Jensen

"I thought Artsy-Fartsy was a great book. Every time we had to take a break reading it, I kept on thinking about what was going to happen next."
- Anna

"I can't rave enough about Artsy-Fartsy by Karla Oceanak and Kendra Spanjer. It has a little bit of everything—fun pictures, interesting storyline, a little mystery, and memorable characters. And it also has something that will appeal to parents—a good message."
— Julie Peterson, bookingmama blog

"THE BOOK WAS VERY HILARIOUS. IT MADE US LAUGH OUT LOUD. YOU HAVE THE BEST CHARACTERS EVER!"
- Sebastian

"Thanks for Artsy-Fartsy. I thought it was a great idea to incorporate new vocabulary into the story to make it interesting and educational. The story made me think of some of my fondest childhood memories, too. The author is really good at relating to kids. We'll be looking forward to the next one."
- Beth

"Artsy-Fartsy is the best book I have read. It is a very hilarious book."
- Mattias

"The first book in an alphabetical series, Artsy-Fartsy is a comic novel starring a 10-year-old Colorado boy who is given a sketchbook by his grandmother to record all his 'artsy -fartsy' ideas. What ensues is a funny, appealing cartoon story with lots of opportunities for Aldo's artsy-fartsy journaling and doodling. Even though being artsy is uncool, Aldo fills his sketchbook with funny, flip, zingy drawings and ideas and makes some headway in figuring out just who he really is after all. The wonderful "A" Word Gallery in the back only makes its audience anticipate the next cool book in the Aldo Zelnick epic series."
- Midwest Book Review

"My students and I are really enjoying *Artsy-Fartsy*. I think the children can identify with Aldo. I introduced *Artsy-Fartsy* to the other fourth grade grammar and composition teacher, and she has used the book as well. We like to use good literature in our teaching, and this year we used *Artsy-Fartsy* to emphasize 'voice' to our students. We also asked the students to identify thoughts and emotions used in the story. We are looking forward to the continuing adventures of Aldo, his friends and family."
- Carol Gorman

"My class and I loved Artsy-Fartsy.
It was the best book of 3rd grade."
- Tanner

"I was completely charmed by this novel. The drawings and text have the quality of simultaneously being appealing to children and also amusing for adults. A big strength here is in the development of the characters. This is wonderful, since this is going to be an A to Z series and we'll have plenty of time to get to know them better. These are individuals with staying power. With the sketchbook comes a wonderful, not-overstated message of allowing Aldo to be himself and follow his creativity. Bravo!"
- Jean Hanson

"Karla Oceanak delivers an entertaining story full of humor, true-to-life characters, and a bit of a mystery. Spanjer's accompanying illustrations complement the storyline with literal characters sketches. I'll admit that I was a bit concerned that there might be some bathroom humor in the book, with a title like *Artsy-Fartsy*. Fear not, there's nothing offensive! In fact, artsy-fartsy is one of the fifty words beginning with the letter A that Aldo introduces to his readers. They're used naturally in the storyline, not forced to fit, and are included in a fun illustrated glossary in the back pages of the book. Three people in my family read the book— my 7-year-old daughter, 12-year-old son, and 40-something Mom; we all got something different from it: daughter enjoyed new vocabulary and word games (goodbye in six languages, pangrams for typing practice), son enjoyed an artistic protagonist (like him), Mom enjoyed giving it her stamp of approval. We're all looking forward to the next book, *Bogus!*"
— Dawn Rennert, sheistoofondofbooks blog

Bogus

AN ALDO ZELNICK COMIC NOVEL

Written by Karla Oceanak

Illustrated by Kendra Spanjer

BAILIWICK PRESS

*Also by Karla Oceanak
and Kendra Spanjer —*
Artsy-Fartsy

This is a work of fiction. Names, characters, places, and incidents are either the product of the author's imagination or are used fictitiously. Any resemblance to actual persons, living or dead, events, or locales is entirely coincidental.

Published by:
Bailiwick Press
309 East Mulberry Street
Fort Collins, Colorado 80524
(970) 672-4878
Fax: (970) 672-4731
www.bailiwickpress.com
www.aldozelnick.com

Book design by:
Launie Parry
Red Letter Creative
www.red letter creative.com

Manufactured by:
Friesens Corporation, Altona, Canada
October 2010
Job # 59977

ISBN 978-1-934649-06-0

Library of Congress Control Number: 2010927959

18 17 16 15 14 13 12 11 10   7 6 5 4 3 2

Dear Aldo –
Your cartooning
skills are bona fide.*
There's still plenty of
summer vacation left, so
be your brilliant self!
Love ya bunches,
Goosy

ALDO,

You accomplished the As.
Now bring on the Bs!
Bon voyage!*

Mr. Mot

WHO'S WHO

GOOSY, MY GRANDMA. ARTIST AND BOHEMIAN.* GIVES ME THESE BLANK SKETCHBOOKS TO WRITE AND DRAW IN. THINKS I'M ARTSY-FARTSY.

MY DAD. MAKES CAKES AND OTHER TASTY SNACKS IN HIS SPARE TIME.

MY MOM. BIG ON ME GETTING EXERCISE. TAKES PICTURES OF BIRDS.

MY DOG, MAX

TIMOTHY, MY SUPER-JOCK BROTHER. HE'S 14.

ME – ALDO ZELNICK. 10 YEARS OLD. HATES PHYSICAL ACTIVITY. LOVES FOOD, TV & VIDEO GAMES. DRAWS.

JACK. SERIOUS ROCK HOUND AND MY BEST FRIEND.

BEE. TREE CLIMBER, FAST RUNNER. BESPECTACLED* GIRL.

BEE'S LITTLE SIS, VIVI.

BEE'S MOM, MRS. GOODE. (FITTING.)

MY TEACHERY NEIGHBOR, MR. MOT. IT WAS HIS IDEA TO PUT HARD, ALPHABETICAL WORDS IN MY SKETCHBOOKS.

JACK'S STINKY DOG, SLATE.

TOMMY GELLER. NEIGHBORHOOD BULLY AND MY ARCHENEMY.

BEE'S CATS, PING AND PONG.

(This is my second sketchbook. I filled up the first one last month and called it *Artsy-Fartsy*. Weird. Anyway, you might want to read it to find out how this whole alphabetical sketchbook thing got started.)

WHEN YOU SEE THIS *,
LOOK IN THE WORD
GALLERY AT THE END OF THIS
SKETCHBOOK. IT TELLS YOU
WHAT THE WORD MEANS.

B IS FOR...
BLOCKHEAD*

At least now I know how to begin <u>this</u> sketchbook...

I'll start by admitting it: I bungled* this whole ring thing.

I botched* it.

I blew it.

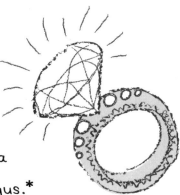

Jack and I found a ring, and I thought it was a fake. I was <u>sure</u> it was bogus.*

11

So I goofed around with it...and I LOST it.

And now I have to find it again. Because it turns out it was real. And there's a $1,000 reward.

Things I could buy with $1,000:

- 893 taquitos
  (the best snack food of all time)

- 250 packs of Pokémon cards

YES! → - 555 40-ounce Slushies

- a big flat-screen TV for my bedroom

MY PRECIOUS

Here's how it began.
It was a couple of weeks ago...

Jack and I were playing kick the rock. That's where Jack grabs some random road rock and kicks it down the street. Then it's my turn to kick it. You get the idea. It's a game that involves moving my body, so it's not my favorite, but Jack is a rock hound, which means he's crazy about rocks, and he's my best friend...sooo yeaaah.

THIS IS ME, REMEMBERING WHAT HAPPENED... (WHY DOES TRYING HARD TO REMEMBER SOMETHING ALMOST ALWAYS INVOLVE WEIRD MOUTH MOTIONS? TRY IT!)

OH YEAH, AND THESE WAVY LINES MEAN THAT THIS STUFF HAPPENED A WHILE AGO.

That's when I kicked the rock and it tumbled down into the storm grate.

"Welp, guess we're done with that game!" I said.

But Jack ran to the gutter and dropped to his belly. "Hey!" he said.

"Oh, c'mon. It's just a rock!" (Of course, I know that to Jack there's no such thing as "just a rock.")

So I got down on my hands and knees and peered into the grate too. Alongside our boring old kicking rock sat something sparkle-shiny.

Slushie money! That's what I was thinking. But then Jack reached down and grabbed the kicking rock.

HEY! GET THE SHINY THING.

I WILL. BUT I HAVE TO SAVE THE ROCK FIRST.

Then he reached down again and pulled out a giant, fakey-looking ring, like the kind you hate getting in those machines that take quarters near the grocery store entrance.

"Well that's <u>obviously</u> bogus," I said, and I plucked the ring from Jack's hand and tossed it back into the gutter.

Jack had just put his magnifying glass to his eye to get a better look at the ring. He isn't usually the kind of guy who goes ballistic,* but at that moment his huge eye was sure glaring at me.

He reached down into the gutter and retrieved the ring again.

"Watcha got there?" said an awfully familiar voice. It was Tommy Geller, the neighborhood bully. He was riding by on his bike and stopped to see what we were doing.

Jack had the ring right up next to his face. He was so absorbed that he didn't even hear Tommy.

"Nothin'," I said. "Just a bogus toy ring some kid must've dropped."

"Hmph," said Tommy. It sounded like a grunt an ape would make. "You should give it to me."

So Jack handed something to Tommy. I thought he was giving him the ring, but instead he gave him our kicking rock.

"What the heck's this?" said Tommy.

"It's a nice piece of marble," said Jack. "Probably from somebody's garden. See the glittery crystals in it?"

The funny thing about Tommy is that he's a rock hound too. Even though he acts all tough and cool, he's a softy when it comes to rocks. And the kicking rock seemed to distract him. He grunted again, shoved the rock into his pocket, and biked away.

ROCK SPARKLY.
ME LIKE.

"Whew, that was close," said Jack, and he went back to examining the ring.

Me, I kept walking. I wanted to get out of the July sun and into the shade of our fort under the giant Colorado Blue Spruce tree.

"¡Hala! What if it's real!" Jack called to me. (Jack's mom is bilingual.* Jack kinda is too. ¡Hala! means something like Holy cow!)

"It's not real!" I yelled back. "That's dumb!"

Like I said, Jack loves rocks. He knows a lot about rocks of all kinds, including gemstones. So maybe when Jack got that squirmy, holy-cow feeling the first time he saw the ring, I should have been a better best friend and listened to him.

HELLO, THIS IS YOURSELF, CALLING FROM THE FUTURE. LISTEN TO JACK!

THE FOG TEST

Bee was in the fort, waiting for us. She's the new kid we hang out with sometimes, even though she's basically a girl.

I plopped down to rest, and Bee handed me the lunchbox we keep in the fort to store our stuff. Inside was a pencil and the brand-new, blank sketchbook my artsy grandma, Goosy, had given me—the very one I'm now writing in.

SKETCHBOOK B WHEN IT WAS STILL BLANK.

WIND-UP TEETH TOY WE FOUND AT THE POOL.

NOTE TO SELF: BRING SNACKS TO KEEP IN LUNCHBOX. WHAT'S A LUNCHBOX WITHOUT FOOD IN IT, ANYWAY?

It had been a couple of weeks since I'd
finished filling up the A sketchbook. Summer
vacation was almost half over, and both
Goosy and Mr. Mot had been asking me how
the second sketchbook was coming along.
"Oh, it's fine," I kept saying. I didn't want to
admit that I hadn't started it yet. I was only
on B, and already I had cartoonist's block.*

So I was sitting there trying to think of something to write or draw. But instead I kept thinking about whether to get a) a taquito and a Slushie or b) a doughnut and a Slushie when we went to the convenience store later.

And then I noticed that Jack was kissing the ring.

"What?! Are you actually smooching that thing?" I asked.

"No, I'm breathing on it," Jack said.

"OK...because rings enjoy...peanut butter breath?" (You know how some kids bring peanut butter sandwiches to school every single day in their lunchboxes? That's Jack. Plain peanut butter sandwiches for lunch ad nauseum, even during summer vacation.)

"No, because one way to tell if it's a diamond is to breathe on it. A diamond won't fog up."

"Look! It's not fogging up!" said Bee.

"Nope," said Jack.

"Ah c'mon," I said. "There's no way that thing is real. Besides, am I the only one who can hear my stomach growling? Let's go get taquitos...or doughnuts...or taquitos..."

WHICH WOULD YOU CHOOSE?

Jack shrugged. "Well, I guess it <u>is</u> unlikely we'd find a real diamond in the gutter. Plus, it <u>does</u> look a lot like the toy ring I gave Sasha when I was little."

Sasha is the girly-girl who lives next door to Jack. When he was 5 and she was 7, he asked her to marry him. Fortunate<u>ly</u> she said no.

HE'S NICE, BUT HE'S NO PRINCE CHARMING.

"Let's just put the ring in the lunchbox for now," said Bee. "Time to race. Last one to the convenience store is a dung beetle!"

Sigh.

ISN'T THERE ANYTHING ELSE ON THE MENU?

ONE FISH, BLUE FISH

The next day my dad and I took our dog, Max, to the pet store to buy him some food and get him a bath. Except at the pet store they don't call it a "bath." They call it "grooming," like it's so fancy a butler* has to do it or something. Sheesh.

While Max was getting "groomed," Dad and I checked out all the weird little creatures you can buy at the pet store, like bearded dragons* and boas.* (Not the fire-blowing kind or the feather kind, as it turned out.)

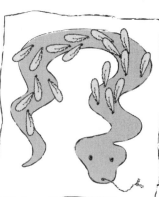

Then I saw this blue fish all by himself in a glass bowl. He was just sitting there, slowly swishing his big, flowy tail back and forth. The sign said he was a betta* fish and that betta fish just like to hang out and barely move.

Yo, WHASSUP?

"Can I get it?" I asked Dad.

"A fish?" Dad said, looking at me askance. "Since when did you become interested in fish?"

"Since I found a fish who's <u>awesome</u> and just like me."

"Hm," said Dad, reading the sign. "Looks like all you have to do is feed it fish food and change the water once in a while. I guess you can buy it with your allowance."

My allowance! In the summer, my allowance is for Slushies. But this <u>would</u> be an uber-cool pet...

So I paid for the betta fish while Dad picked up Max from the grooming room. Poor Max.

A BOW! DAD, TAKE OFF THE BOW. WE CAN'T TAKE HIM OUT IN PUBLIC LOOKING LIKE THAT.

MAXIE BOY! THEY GAVE YOU A BOUFFANT!*

After we got home, I took the betta fish up to my room and cleared off a spot on my table. I set his bowl there, and we spent some time getting to know each other.

I thought that his bowl looked awfully blah.* Even though betta fish are supposed to <u>like</u> living alone in a small bowl, I figured he'd like it better with a little bric-a-brac,* right? So I biked down to the fort, grabbed the bogus ring from the lunchbox, came home, and plunked it into the fishbowl. There. That was better.

A LONG DAY'S JOURNEY

Summer vacation is the best possible thing that could ever happen. But even I have to admit that sometimes it gets a tiny bit banal.*

A few more days had passed, and Jack had been gone with his dad. Bee was probably climbing a tree somewhere, all the TV cartoons were reruns, and I was bored. I made the big-time mistake of telling my mom.

"I'm bored," I said. ← MOM WARNING!

NEVER say those two words to your parents, especially not to your mother.

OH GOOD. GO GET THE LAUNDRY OUT OF THE DRYER AND FOLD IT. AND DON'T FORGET TO CLEAN OUT THE LINT FILTER.

I groaned, but I knew better than to complain. Complaining would only lose me all screen time for the rest of the day. So I folded the dumb laundry.

"Look, Max. Does this make you feel better?"

"Keep wearing those on your head for the next month and we'll be even."

Then I scooped the fuzzy, warm gob of lint from the dryer's filter. It felt so soft and nice that I decided to keep it. I stuffed it into my pocket.

WHY DOES BELLYBUTTON LINT SMELL DIFFERENT THAN THE DRYER KIND?

Still bored, I walked over to Mr. Mot's house to see what he was doing.

He was sitting cross-legged on his front porch with his palms face-up on his knees. His eyes were closed, and he was humming softly to himself.

"Hello, Aldooo..." Mr. Mot hummed flatly without opening his eyes. "Come empty your minnnd...Join meee..."

Welp, can't be any more boring than sitting at home, I thought. So I criss-cross-applesauced next to Mr. Mot, touched my pointer fingers to my thumbs, and closed my eyes too.

I was wrong about meditating being less boring than sitting at home. "Mr. Mottt...I am so borrred..." I chanted. "This isn't helpinggg..."

Mr. Mot clapped twice and jumped to his feet. I tried to do the same but fell back onto my butt.

"How is your B sketchbook coming along?" he asked, helping me to my feet.

"Um. Fine," I lied.

"I'm reading a biography of Charles Schulz," said Mr. Mot. "He's the man who drew the Snoopy and Charlie Brown comics all those years. He was one of the world's greatest cartoonists."

Yup. Still bored, I thought.

"Charles Schulz earned not only beaucoup* admiration and satisfaction from his work, but also a great deal of money, Aldo. Did you know that he started drawing comic strips when he was just a boy?"

A lot of money...from comic strips! Now *that* was an unboring idea.

"See ya, Mr. Mot!" I said, and I hurried back home.

Quiz: Where is the ring right now?

Answer: In the fishbowl!

34

BACON BOY

When I got there, Dad was making breakfast burritos, even though it was lunchtime. Yumbo! So while he cooked, I sat down at the kitchen counter to start inventing my own comic strip.

I got out a few loose pieces of paper and a pencil. I drew some blank squares in a row...the kind comics get drawn in. I pulled the lint ball from my pocket and played with it. I chewed on my pencil. I tried to balance it on my nose.

EVERYTHINGS BETTER WITH BACON

Here's the thing: It's <u>hard</u> creating characters and a story out of thin air. Plus, Timothy, my dumb big brother, was distracting me. He was walking around the kitchen juggling and generally being a bother. He likes to show off his athletic abilities.

I closed my eyes and thought, thought, thought. I remembered that Goosy always tells me to do what I love. What do I love that I could turn into a comic strip? I rested my head on the counter and opened my eyes. Dad was just setting down a plateful of crispy-cooked bacon. Boing!

Bacon! That was it!

I got busy drawing. Here's the character I came up with:

I'M A SUPER-HERO WITH SIZZLE! A PROTEIN PACKED WITH POWER! I'M BACON BOY!

Dad, Timothy, and I pigged out on breakfast burritos. Mmm! I showed them Bacon Boy and explained how my new comic strip was gonna make me rich and famous, just like Charles Schulz.

Then the phone rang. It was Jack, calling from his dad's cell phone. He was on his way home. He asked me to get the ring and bring it to his Mom-house because he wanted to take a closer look at it. I didn't tell him the ring was, at that very moment, keeping my new betta fish company.

"Okay," I said. "I'll see you in a little bit." And I went up to my room to feed my betta-fish-with-no-name and get the ring from his bowl. My hands still had some bacon crumbs on them, so the fish got a special treat for breakfast that day too.

BOK CHOY
AND BHUTAN

I got on my bike and started off for Jack's house, the ring tucked safely in my pocket. I guessed that he probably wouldn't be home for a few more minutes, so I pedaled past Bee's house. Her little sister, Vivi, was blowing bubbles in the driveway, and she beckoned* for me to follow her into the backyard. (Vivi doesn't say much, but she always seems to know what's going on.)

There was Bee, digging in her vegetable garden.

"Oh hi there," she said. "What are you doing today? Come try some bok choy.*"

"I'm just bringing that bogus ring to Jack," I said. I showed it to Bee then set it on the edge of the garden bed so my hands were free. I pulled off a leaf of the lettucey vegetable Bee was pointing at and nibbled on a piece. It tasted bitter,* like cabbage. Blech.

Just then Bee's mom came out the back door of the house with a big jar in her hand. "Aldo!" she said. "We're helping place these collection jars around town. The children of Bhutan* need our help."

YOUR SPARE CHANGE CAN FEED A HUNGRY CHILD!

My first thought: Bhutan? It sorta rhymed with futon, but I'd never heard of it.

pennies for Bhutan

My second thought: I need my spare change... for Slushies!

"My pen-pal lives in Bhutan. It's a little country in Asia, between China and India," explained Bee. "She only gets one full meal a day, and that's at school. So my family decided to help."

Bee and Vivi and their mom all looked at me with their big, girly eyes.

I thought about my breakfast burrito and how full I was. But I also thought about the Slushie I would be buying later that afternoon.

"Um, I don't really have any extra money with me right now..." I said. "I could probably give some later..."

Mrs. Goode lifted one eyebrow and said, "OK. Better late than never!"

"Uh, sure," I said, feeling the tiniest bit guilty. "I gotta go to Jack's now." I reached in my pocket for the ring then remembered I'd set it near the garden. But it was gone. Vivi was pointing at a new garden sign she'd made.

YOU REAP WHAT YOU SOW!

NICE! NOW I CAN FINALLY PROPOSE TO MY GIRLFRIEND!

"Hey, gimme the ring," I said to Vivi. I glared at her and held out my hand.

Bee blithely* troweled the ring out of the loose dirt and handed it to me, and I took it to Jack's.

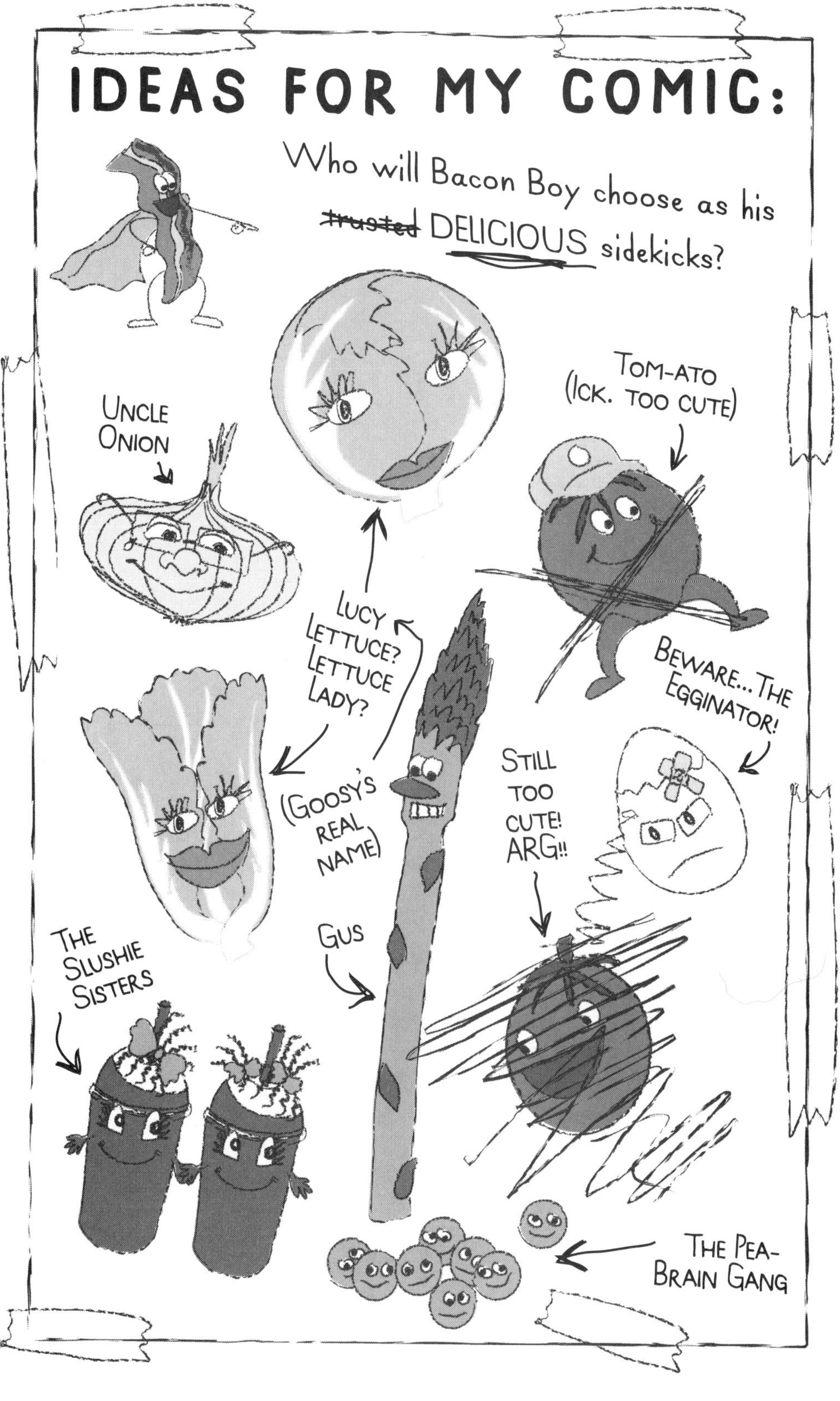

IDEAS FOR MY COMIC:
Who will Bacon Boy choose as his ~~trusted~~ DELICIOUS sidekicks?
UNCLE ONION
TOM-ATO (ICK. TOO CUTE)
LUCY LETTUCE? LETTUCE LADY?
(GOOSY'S REAL NAME)
BEWARE...THE EGGINATOR!
STILL TOO CUTE! ARG!!
GUS
THE SLUSHIE SISTERS
THE PEA-BRAIN GANG

JACK GETS
LOUPE-Y

Jack was in his room at his Mom-house waiting for me.

Jack's bedroom is his rock room. Actually, since Jack lives in 2 different houses—one with his mom and one with his dad—he has 2 rock rooms. He keeps his sedimentary rocks at his mom's house and his igneous and metamorphic rocks at his dad's house. Rocks are totally his bailiwick.*

BRECCIA

"How was your trip to..."

Jack didn't even give me a chance to finish my question. "Didja bring the ring?"

"Yes, I brought the dumb ring." I pulled it from my pocket and handed it to him. It had some dirt, lint, and fish-food flakes clinging to it.

Jack gasped. "What have you been doing with it?"

"Don't go berserk.* It's just a bogus toy."

I followed Jack into his bathroom, where he filled the sink with warm water and a squirt of soap. Then he gave the ring a bath! He used an old toothbrush to remove all the dirt from the nooks and crannies. He even blew it dry with a hairdryer.

Back in his bedroom, Jack turned on the lamp on his worktable and looked at the ring through this little lens thing. It's called a loupe (it rhymes with ~~poop~~ soup). It's basically a super-duper magnifying glass.

"Very square-cut facets," Jack murmured. "Excellent clarity. It scratches glass. And when I put this piece of newspaper beneath it...I can't read the words!"

He crossed his arms and turned to me with a dramatic look of satisfaction, as if he had proven his point beyond a shadow of a doubt.

"Uh....yeaaah," I said.

"Aldo, this ring is passing all the tests! It's a <u>real</u> diamond. It's gotta be pretty valuable. What should we do with it?"

For the first time I had a blip* of a feeling that Jack could be right.

"Let's show it to my mom," he said.

"No! If it's real, which it probably isn't, she'd auction it on eBay!" I said. Jack's mom, Mrs. Lopez, makes money by selling things on eBay. "Let's show it to Mr. Mot."

Jack nodded. Mr. Mot is our go-to guy when we need good advice.

"How valuable is valuable?" I asked. "If we found a <u>real</u> diamond ring like this, could we sell it for enough money to buy, say, a nice flat-screen TV?"

Just then Mrs. Lopez popped her head into the room. "Time for your dentist appointment, Jack!"

Jack and I both jumped a mile. I grabbed the ring and stuffed it back into my pocket.

"OK, Aldo," Jack whispered. "Your mission is to take the ring to Mr. Mot and see what he says. Be very careful not to lose it."

"I won't lose it. Sheesh!" I whispered back. Yeah, right.

WHAT?! IT'S NOT LIKE I'M CARELESS!

THE THRILL OF VICTORY

I biked straight to Mr. Mot's house, but he wasn't there! Dang it.

So I went home and sat at the kitchen counter again. Timothy juggled by, this time with eggs. Sheesh he was getting good. I thought about showing him the ring, but generally speaking, big brothers can't be trusted.

While I waited for Mr. Mot to come home, I got out my Bacon Boy sketch and worked on it some more. Bee's garden had given me a great idea:

BACON BOY battles Voracio

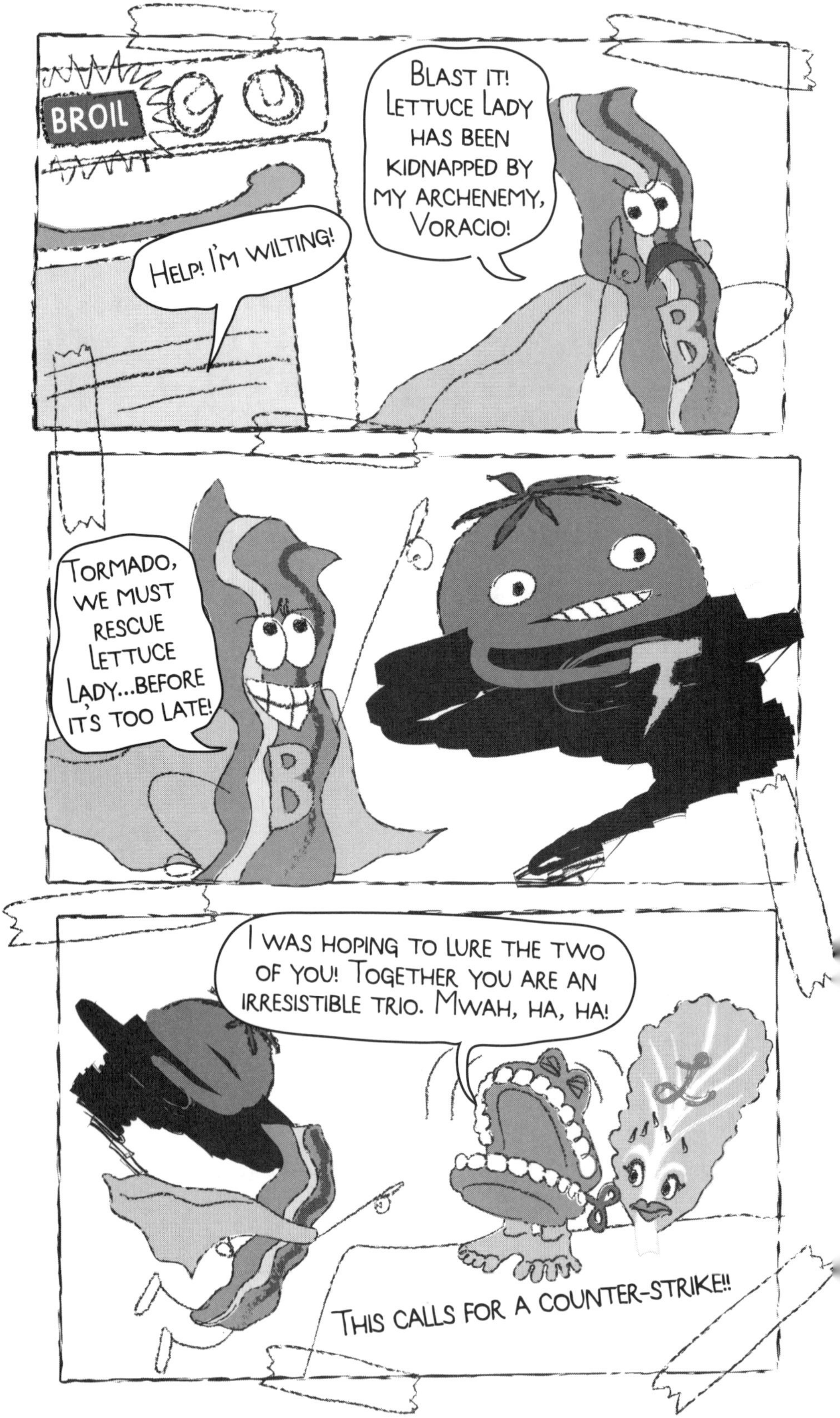
BROIL
HELP! I'M WILTING!
BLAST IT! LETTUCE LADY HAS BEEN KIDNAPPED BY MY ARCHENEMY, VORACIO!
TORMADO, WE MUST RESCUE LETTUCE LADY...BEFORE IT'S TOO LATE!
I WAS HOPING TO LURE THE TWO OF YOU! TOGETHER YOU ARE AN IRRESISTIBLE TRIO. MWAH, HA, HA!
THIS CALLS FOR A COUNTER-STRIKE!!

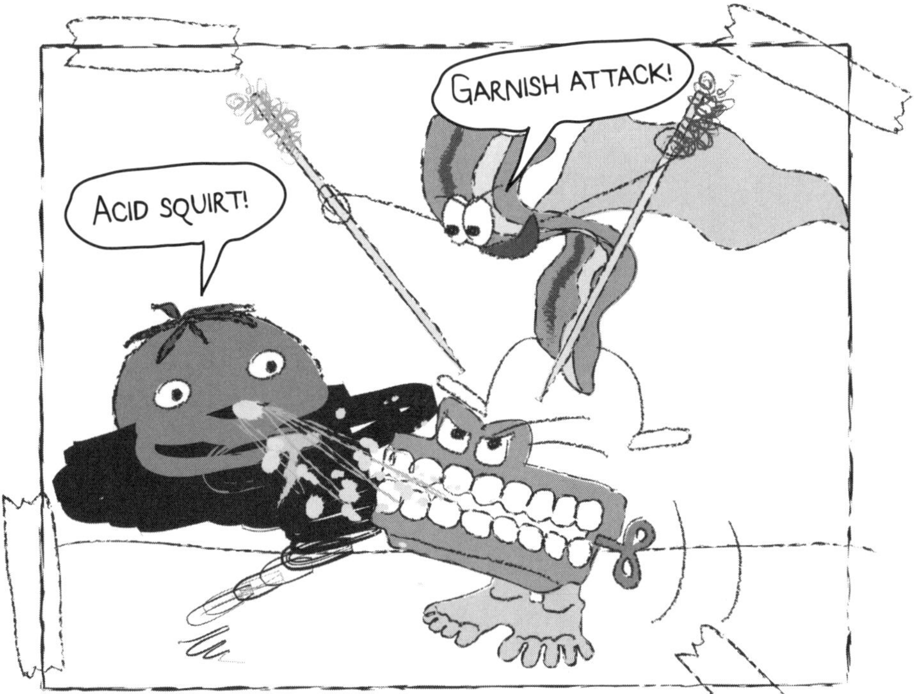
ACID SQUIRT!
GARNISH ATTACK!

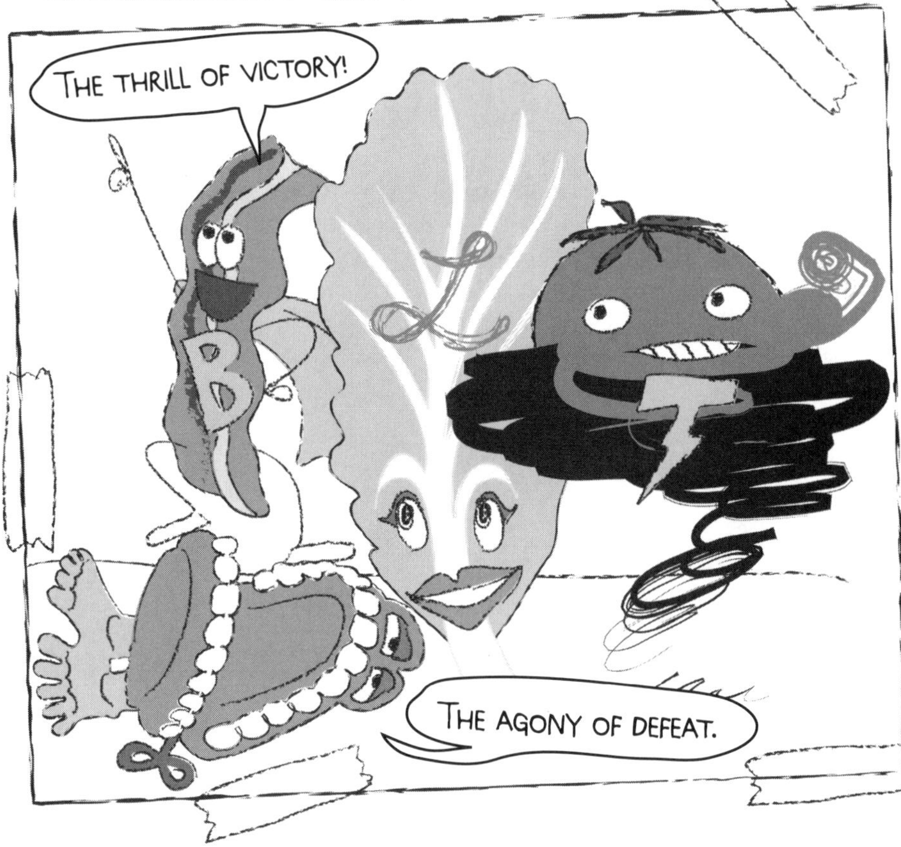
THE THRILL OF VICTORY!
THE AGONY OF DEFEAT.

POOPER SCOOPER

By the time I looked up from my first finished comic strip, an hour or 2 had passed. Mr. Mot, I remembered. I was just sliding off my stool to amble over to his house when my mom walked into the kitchen.

"Going to Mr. Mot's!" I said on my way out the door.

"Not so fast!" she said. "Did you scoop poop?"

"Ugh," I groaned. "It's Timothy's turn."

"Nope. Check the chart!" she said.

My mom had created a chart for our summer chores and posted it prominently on the kitchen cupboard.

"OK, I'll do it later," I promised.

"If by later you mean NOW, that's perfect."

As I've said before, it's a bad idea to argue with my mom. So I got a bag and shovel and went to the backyard to pick up dog poop.

Have you ever scooped poop on a broiling*
hot day in July? It's disgusting. The new
poops are gooey-soft, and they stink. Some
baby barf* gurgled into my mouth.

If you can ignore the smell, though, and
where they come from, dog doodies are
kinda interesting. I mean, sometimes you
can tell what your dog has been eating just
by looking at them. Max eats the craziest
things.

LEGO

CANDY WRAPPER

SHOELACE

SCRABBLE LETTER

I had just finished bagging the poop when
Mom joined me in the backyard. "Oh good,
you're still here!" she said. "It's a beautiful
day OUTSIDE. You need some more FRESH
AIR. Come over here in the shade with me,
and let's do some yoga."

I've mentioned that when my mom says OUTSIDE and FRESH AIR, she means exercise. She thinks that since I'm still carrying around a little baby fat* and I don't like sports, she needs to invent ways for me to move around.

I folded my arms and frowned at her.

"Aldo, yoga is more like meditation than exercise. Mr. Mot told me you tried meditating with him. It's similar, only with some stretching mixed in."

Stretching, huh. I AM pretty flexible, I thought. "All right, I'll try it."

So Mom taught me how to start in the lotus position, which is just like meditating.

Then we moved into the Camel pose. I could see Timothy stringing a rope between two trees in our backyard.

HEY TIMOTHY! I FOUND A SPORT I'M BETTER AT THAN YOU ARE!

I AM THE KING OF AWESOMENESS.

Next we did the King of the Dance pose. That one was harder because I had to balance on one foot, first my right then my left.

X-RAY VIEW: THE RING WAS IN MY POCKET DURING YOGA.

By now Timothy had tied the rope tight and was up in the tree, holding an old broomstick.

The last pose I tried was the Eagle. "This is dumb," I said. "It should be called the 'I Have to Pee.'"

I watched Timothy tightrope walk across the backyard, grinning like the Cheshire Cat.

"Yup, that's enough FRESH AIR for me!" I said. "I'm going to Mr. Mot's." And I took off, leaving Timothy and Mom to their balancing acts in our backyard.

MY PRECIOUS II

Mr. Mot STILL wasn't there, so I went back home and called Jack to say we should go swimming until Mr. Mot got home. It was hot, and I was sweaty, which I <u>do not</u> enjoy.

I put the ring in the pocket of my swim trunks and walked down to the neighborhood pool to meet Jack. As soon as I spotted him, I held up the ring so he could see it...then I tossed it into the pool.

"Nooo!" cried Jack.

"What? It's a rock, isn't it?" Sheesh.

We'd been playing dive-for-the-rock at the swimming pool ever since forever!

OWIE! THIS SLUSHIE IS GIVING ME A BABY BRAIN FREEZE!*

But Jack was already in the water, swimming after his precious ring. So I jumped in after him. (He beat me to it, of course. Jack always wins at dive-for-the-rock.) After that, Jack had to agree that racing for a maybe-diamond is way more exciting than racing for just any old rock, so we kept playing dive-for-the-ring until I got tired.

Finally it was Slushie time. Jack and I are Slushie aficionados. Almost every day in the summer we cool off with Slushies from the convenience store near our house.

Bee was at the pool too and came with us. But when we got to the convenience store, she decided to save her coins for the Bhutan jar. "I got a letter from my pen-pal yesterday," Bee said. "She wrote that every day she looks forward to the rice they serve at her school for lunch." Bee looked intently at me again with those big, girly eyes.

Me, I got a Slushie. Hey, I deserved a treat! I'd meditated, created a comic strip, scooped poop, learned yoga, and gone swimming...and it was only 4 o'clock in the afternoon!

"So, what are you guys gonna do with the ring?" asked Bee.

"We're going to show it to Mr. Mot," Jack said. "Aldo, you have the ring, right?"

"Yeah, maybe Mr. Mot is finally home," I said. "Let's go see." I reached into the pocket of my swim trunks to show Jack that of course I had the ring...but it wasn't there. "Uh-oh," I said. "I think...uh...maybe I...uh... we...left it...at the pool."

"Whaaa?" Jack said. He looked and sounded like he was strangling.

The 3 of us made a beeline* back to the pool, and there was the ring, right next to my goggles, which were right next to big feet with hairy toes, which were connected to... Tommy Geller!

Bee is the fastest runner on my baseball team. I used to think this was annoying, since I'm the slowest runner. But this time her speediness came in awfully handy.

She bolted* over to Tommy and screeched to a stop right next to him. But she must have actually bumped him just the eensiest bit, because just as he was leaning over to grab the ring, he toppled into the swimming pool. She's brazen!*

HEY! I WAS JUST STANDING. NOW I'M FALLING!

THE BIGGER THEY ARE, THE HARDER THEY FALL.

POOF!

Jack and Bee and I took the ring to Mr. Mot's house and climbed the steps to his front porch.

We rang the doorbell. He wasn't home!!!

I sat down. It was beginning to feel like the longest day of my life. I was tired. And I was tired of trying to find Mr. Mot.

OH GEEZ! I WAS ACCIDENTALLY ACTIVE TODAY!

"OK. Time for Plan B," I said. "Let's go to my house. My dad will know what to do about this dumb ring." Bee handed me the ring, and I stuck it on my thumb. It looked totally bogus.

A few minutes later we burst into my kitchen. There was my dad, making a blueberry cake! (My dad loves to make cakes. And I love to eat his cakes.)

"Mr. Zelnick," said Jack. "We have something very important to show you."

Timothy was standing next to my dad. He was holding an...upside-down top hat?! "Hey Aldo, now I'm learning how to make things disappear," he said.

Max was sitting on one of the counter stools, begging for a lick of cake batter.

"Mr. Zelnick, it's time for Plan Bee," said Bee, peeking into Timothy's top hat.

"You kids look half-starved," said my dad, ignoring what everyone was saying. "Hop up here, and I'll make you a snack."

It's bedlam* in here, I thought.

I still don't know exactly what happened next, and I want you to keep in mind that cake was being made <u>right</u> <u>there</u> in front of me. It's <u>so easy</u> to get distracted when baked goods are involved!

Here's what I do know. It all happened in a split second: Jack tripped on Max's squeak toy. Max jumped over the counter after it, tipping the flour canister and sending a puffy cloud of whiteness into the air. I startled and grabbed the counter, accidentally smooshing my hand into the bowl of blueberries. And Timothy shouted, "Abracadabra!"

And just like that, the ring was gone.

"Where's the ring, Aldo?" squeaked Jack.

"I must've dropped it," I said. "But it's gotta be right here. I just had it."

"What ring?" asked Dad.

While Bee and Jack and I searched through the mess, we told my dad about the ring and how we found it and how Jack had done all these geological tests on it to tell if it was a bona fide diamond or not.

A bona fide diamond. Saying it out loud to a grown-up made me feel dumb. How could a ring we had found in the gutter and played with for the last few days possibly be real? I looked over at Jack and noticed that his face was kind of red. I could tell he was bummed.*

My dad made us feel better, though. He gave us each a little bowl of blueberries and a glass of ice water with a slice of lemon. While we watched, he gave the cake batter a stir with a wooden spoon to show us there was nothing in it, then he poured it into the cake pans and put them into the oven. After that he went about sweeping and mopping the kitchen floor, all the while telling us about the time when he was a kid and he thought a ring he'd gotten in a box of Cracker Jacks was real.

"I tried to sell it to my little brother, Vince," he chuckled, "but my mom—Goosy—made me give him back his money. You kids go relax. I'll keep cleaning up the kitchen, and when I find the ring, we'll all take a good look at it together."

But it didn't turn up. So that's how the bogus ring that was lost then found then almost taken by Tommy Geller then stuck in a fishbowl then planted in a garden then given a bath then scientifically tested then carried along during comic-strip drawing, poop scooping, and yoga then chlorinated then left behind then almost taken by Tommy Geller again (!) then lost one final time came to be the story of my B sketchbook.

THERE IT WAS, IN BLACK AND WHITE

Everything I've told you so far happened in just a few days. And even though Dad and I searched and searched some more, the ring hadn't been found again.

Oh well, I thought. *It was probably a fake anyway.* Once it was lost for good, even Jack seemed to convince himself that the ring must have been bogus.

"I thought for sure it was real," said Jack. "But I guess if someone lost a real diamond like that, there would have been an article in the newspaper or something. *Oh bien.**"

Then this morning, Jack and Bee and I were hanging out in my front yard. Goosy rode up on her bike to visit.

C'MON, ALDO, TRY THE NEW MOVES I LEARNED IN MY BREAKDANCING* CLASS!

UH, I THINK I LEARN BETTER BY WATCHING.

My mom stepped outside with the newspaper in her hands. "Look!" she said. "There's a story in here about a diamond ring that was lost in our neighborhood. It's worth a lot of money, and they're offering a $1,000 reward to anyone who finds it. It's like a treasure hunt! You kids should look for it!"

The newspaper even showed a photo of the ring. There it was, right there in black and white...our not-so-bogus diamond.

"Whaaa?" Jack was doing that strangling thing again.

"A thousand dollars!" said Bee. "Gosh!"

"Aw geez, geez, geez!" I yelled, and I stomped all over the yard. "There goes my flat-screen TV!"

"Goslings!" said Goosy. "What's the problem?"

So we told Goosy and my mom about how we'd found the ring...but then we'd messed around with it and lost it again.

"That ring looked _way_ bogus!" I said. "Jack, c'mon, you should have known better. How could you have let me fool around with a real diamond?"

The mad/sad look Jack gave me at that moment made my chest hurt and my head throb. My heart felt like it might implode—like when I'm _forced_ to run the 50-meter dash at school. And my head felt like it does when I get a brain freeze from drinking my Slushie too fast.

"That is quite a bewildering* story," said Mom. "But the good news is that the ring couldn't have gone too far. If it was in our kitchen when it disappeared, it's still here somewhere."

Then it dawned on me. <u>Of course.</u> "Disappeared!" I said. "Timothy was making things disappear! <u>He</u> has the ring. Let's go get it, guys."

We were all so busy talking about the ring that we hadn't noticed Tommy Geller walking by. But here he was, and by the smirk on his face, I could tell he had overheard our conversation. Blast!*

TIMOTHY TO THE RESCUE (NOT)

Jack and Bee and I raced up to Timothy's bedroom and banged on his door. He didn't answer, so we barged* in. It was almost noon, and he was still asleep!

"Give us the ring, Poodini," I said.

"Grmdlsmsdw," he mumbled. His head was wedged under his pillow.

"C'mon, wake up and give us the ring back!"

YIKES. I DON'T THINK I WANT TO BE A TEENAGER.

IF HE ATE MORE VEGGIES, HE WOULDN'T BE SO TIRED.

YUP. THIS IS MY MENTOR AND PROTECTOR.

Timothy pulled his head out, opened one eye, and growled, "You entered my room. You woke me up. And you brought two of your friends along. How nice."

"You pretended to make our ring disappear, but really you took it. Did you think you could use the reward money to buy a stupid trick rabbit or something? Give it back."

Now Timothy sat up and stretched. We could see tufts of hair under his armpits like the ones on Tommy Geller's toes. Yuck.

"Aldo, I didn't take your stupid ring. Get out."

"Where is it then?"

"I have no bleepity-bleep* idea."

"You have to have it."

"I don't have it!" he yelled, then he yawned so big we could see the dangle-y thing at the back of his throat. Double yuck.

"OK...I have another idea," said Bee. "In all the brouhaha* in the kitchen that day, I _did_ notice Max snarfing down some blueberries and spilled cake batter. I bet the ring got mixed in with some food and he ate it."

And with a snort, Timothy slid his head back beneath his pillow and went to sleep again.

Oh geez. This is not going to be pretty, I thought. Out loud I said, "Poop patrol!" and led my friends into the backyard.

WHERE ANGELS FEAR TO TREAD

I STEPPED IN ONE. ICK!

It seems like I'd just cleaned up after Max and here I stood, looking out on a yard full of little piles. Maybe the neighbors' dogs were sneaking into our backyard, too, and using it as the neighborhood dog-o-potty.

"Jack, you have a dog, so you know why we're here," I said. "Go find a stick and get to work. Bee, if Max swallowed the ring, as you suggest, we're probably going to find it in one of these piles."

"That makes sense," agreed Bee. "It's important we don't miss any, then. I'll climb that tree so I can see everything."

"Well, OK."

So Jack and I poked through poop piles with sticks while Bee shouted directions. "Get that one, over there by the birdbath!" "Oooh, there's a sneaky one, hiding behind the basketball!"

I tried to keep track of everywhere we looked. Still no ring!

Jack's never a blabbermouth,* but he was being uber-quiet. I knew why, and it was time for me to say something about it.

"So, uh...you knew the ring was real all along, huh."

He shrugged and didn't look at me.

"Sorry I didn't believe you. Sheesh." I kicked a dried-up pile and sent it bouncing across the yard. "Cuz now we won't be able to get the giant flat-screen TV we've been wanting for my room!"

Jack finally looked up at me. "We _are_ going to find the ring again, Aldo," he said evenly. "And when we do, _I'm_ going to decide how the reward money will be spent. Got it?"

"OK, OK," I said. _Rocks!_ I thought. _That's what he'll spend the reward money on. Oh joy. Unless Tommy Geller finds the ring before we do, which would be <u>even</u> <u>worse</u>._

We picked through every pile in the backyard but didn't find the ring. I looked over at Max, who was teaching Slate how to do yoga. (I know—weird. But that's what it looked like they were doing—the Happy Baby pose.) I suppose the ring could still be inside Max. I wonder how long it takes for something that goes in to come back out?

After that, Jack and Bee went home, and I played video games for the rest of the day. My mom must have felt sorry for me cuz she let me.

PENNIES IN THE FOUNTAIN

Today, as a treat, my mom took me, Bee, Vivi, Jack, and Timothy downtown to do some shopping. Don't get me wrong...I don't like to "shop." But the old part of our town has cool stores and good snacks, and I like hanging out there. First we went to my favorite ice cream shop and got giant cones. We sat near the fountain and ate them while Mom shopped for a few minutes.

My mom also gave us pennies for the fountain. When I threw mine, I made a wish that somewhere, somehow, we'd find the ring and get our reward money.

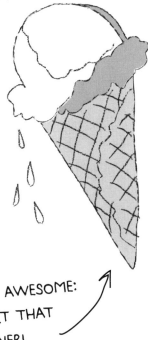

WHY ICE CREAM CONES ARE AWESOME: BECAUSE THEY'RE THE DESSERT THAT COMES IN AN EDIBLE CONTAINER!

Then we went to Asian Emporium. It's a gift shop filled with tons of cool things, like chopsticks and incense and singing bowls.* It has a bazillion* little statues too. Dragons. Lucky cats. Buddhas.*

Goosy likes Buddha. She told me once that he was this guy from India who lived in ancient times. He sat under a tree and meditated for 6 years straight, until he figured out how to be perfectly happy. I would think meditating for 6 years would make you perfectly sore in the butt area.

I WISH TAQUITOS HAD BEEN INVENTED.

Anyway, Goosy says that Buddha tried to teach everyone to be peaceful and not care about "stuff." Like flat-screen TVs. He thought that happiness didn't come from the things in our lives but instead from our thoughts and our behavior* towards others. Obviously he lived before video games and Slushies were invented. In his day the funnest things were probably rock games and a piece of fruit. I'm pretty sure if Buddha were alive today, he would agree that junk food and electronics make true happiness possible.

OOOH, FUN!

What I like about Buddha is how he looks. A lot of the statues show him as this fat, bald guy with a giant smile on his face. It makes you happy just looking at him.

Then in the Asian store today I saw a sign saying that if you rubbed the laughing Buddha's belly, it would bring you good luck! Boy do I need good luck. One of the small laughing Buddha statues only cost 4 bucks, so I borrowed a 5-dollar bill from Timothy to buy it.

RUB HERE FOR LUCK TO FIND RING. (HEY! HOW DID HE GET SO FAT IF HE NEVER HAD JUNK FOOD?)

At the checkout counter at the Asian Emporium sat a Pennies for Bhutan jar. Geez! They were everywhere! When the clerk handed me my change from the 5-dollar bill, he nudged the jar towards me, but I pretended I didn't notice, and I pocketed the coins.

As we were leaving the store, the clerk called, "Happy karma!" and I walked away thinking that I didn't know what karma was, but  it sounded like caramel and at least that was a sweet thing to think about in my misery over the lost reward money.

When I got home I put the little laughing Buddha statue in my betta fish's bowl. He seemed lonely.

JUST CHILLIN' WITH MY HOMIE.

Oh yeah, and Bee wanted to draw about our day too...

When we were downtown today,

HERE!

I climbed to the top of the fountain and placed my wishing penny on the goose at the very top.

I can't say what I wished, because then it won't come true.

Aldo bought a Buddha that looks a lot like him.

And I saw Jack put some money in the Bhutan jar at the Asian store. Jack is super nice.

THE PERSISTENCE OF MEMORY

Today was another burning hot day.

Jack and Bee and I met in our fort and brainstormed* where the ring could be. Over and over and over again—ad nauseum!—we reviewed how, on the day the ring had disappeared, I'd been wearing it on my thumb when we walked into the kitchen at my house.

"And your dad was baking a cake," said Jack. "Hey, what happened to the cake?"

"He freezes his cakes before he decorates them," I said. "It's probably in our freezer."

"Timothy was practicing magic tricks," said Bee. "And Max was sitting at the counter. Then he jumped and spilled the flour."

"We've looked in the flour," said Jack.

"OK, but what if it sunk into the flour?" I said. "Like, what if it's buried at the bottom of the flour container?"

So we shuffled back to my house and got out the flour container. I stuck my hand into it and felt around. No ring.

Just to be sure, we poured the flour into a sifter and squeezed the handle until all the flour had sifted through into the big bowl we'd put there to catch it.

HELLO! MISERY LOVES COMPANY! YOU GUYS ARE SUPPOSED TO BE MISERABLE TOO!

Still no ring.

"Let's go swimming!" said Bee, trying to cheer me up.

But thinking about swimming brought up memories of the good old days playing dive-for-the-ring, which made me even more bummed.

"I know!" said Bee. "It's so hot, I think we could fry an egg on the sidewalk. Let's try."

"Nobody likes eggs without bacon," I said.

"We're not going to eat the egg, Aldo," said Bee. "It's like a science experiment."

Hm. That sounded cool, but cooking food without eating it also seemed kind of dumb.

"Let's make pancakes instead," I said, tapping the big bowl of flour in front of us. "We practically have pancake mix ready."

So we added a couple of eggs and some water to the bowl and stirred.

"Does it need anything else?" asked Jack.

It looked like pancake batter, but we weren't sure it was right, so we added sugar, salt, vanilla, chocolate chips, and bacon bits. (Because, why not?)

We grabbed a can of spray oil and the batter bowl and walked out to the hottest piece of pavement we could find.

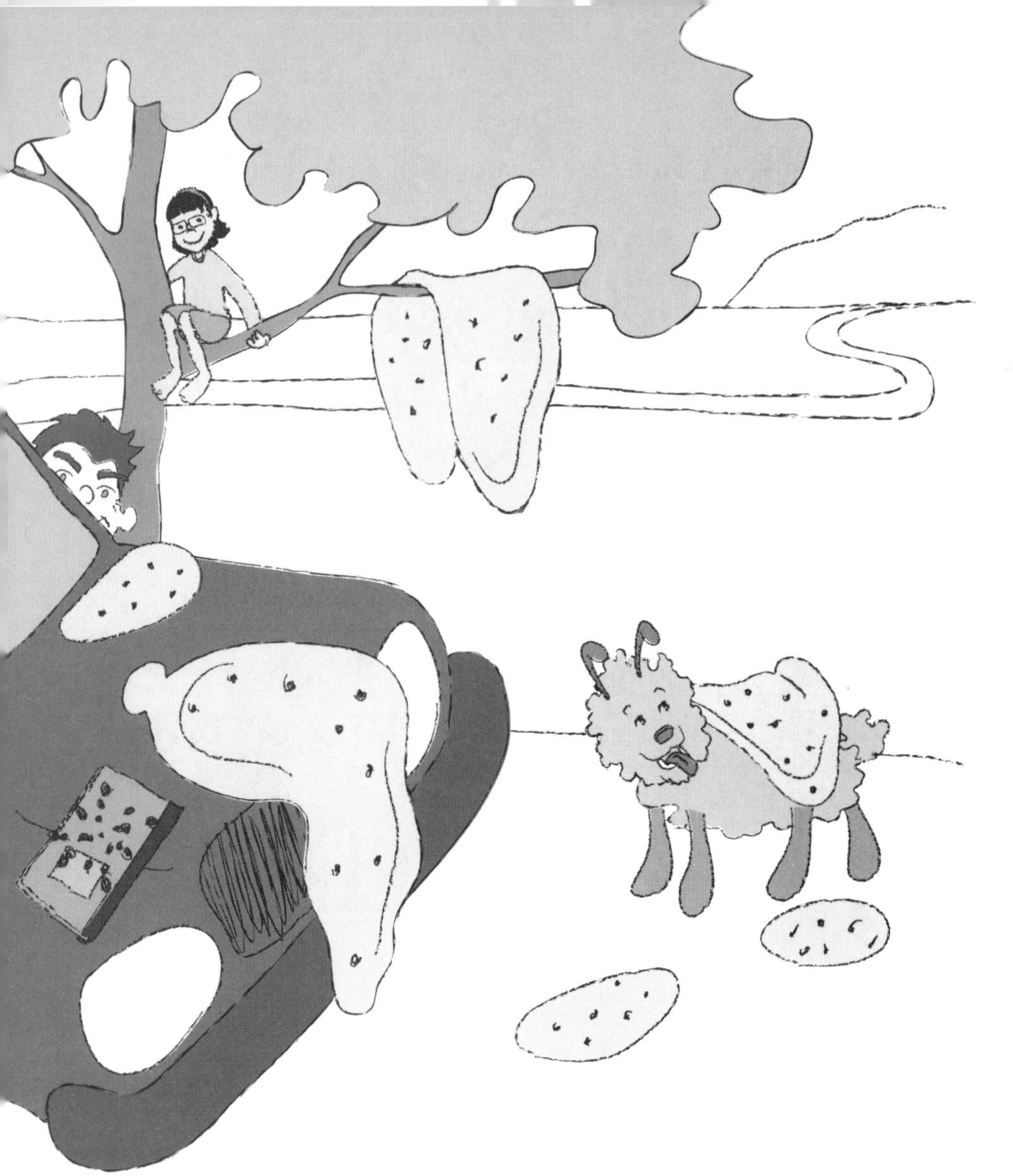

Let's just say our pancake experiment didn't turn out so great, though Max sure seemed to enjoy it. And it did take our minds off the lost ring for an afternoon. I guess when you're bereft,* that's the best you can hope for.

HOW TO MAKE A BUNNY DISAPPEAR

Timothy showed me how to make an object disappear using his magic hat.

1. Get a magic-looking hat and a bunny.

2. If you can't find a real bunny, use a stuffed one.

3. Make a false bottom for your magic hat. Cut a piece of cardboard so it fits snugly down into the bottom of your hat. Paint it or cover it with fabric so it's the same color as the hat.

4. Hide the bunny inside the hat, between the false bottom and the real bottom.

5. Say abracadabra and tap the hat with a magic wand or something bogus like that.

6. Reach into the hat, move aside the false bottom, and grab the bunny by the scruff of the neck. Pull him out to show the audience.

7. Take a bow.

8. Shake your head because this is dumb.

Q: WHAT'S INVISIBLE AND SMELLS LIKE A CARROT?

A: A BUNNY FART.

TEA FOR TWO

Goosy knows I've been feeling blue* about the lost ring, so today she said she'd take me somewhere special.

She had to deliver a few of her paintings to an art gallery in Boulder, which is a city not far from here. So we drove to Boulder, dropped off the paintings, then went to the tea factory for a tour. That's right! A factory where they make tea bags!

First we sat in a little theater where they showed a movie about how farmers all over the world grow the tea leaves and herbs for the teas.

Then, before we went any farther, we had to put hairnets on. That was dumb.

AAACK! THAT LITTLE BLOKE* WHO VISITED THE FACTORY DROPPED A HAIR IN MY TEA!

(SOMETHING THAT WOULD NEVER HAPPEN. C'MON!)

Behind the next door was a real-live factory, not with oompa-loompas but with regular grown-ups running big machines and putting mixtures of nice-smelling things together that ended up in tiny little teabags.

We even got to go into the peppermint room. It's this huge room stacked high with giant bins FULL of peppermint leaves! You know how onions can make your eyes water? Welp, so can uber-mintiness.

After the tour, Goosy and I sat in the tasting room and sampled some of the teas. I put 5 sugar packets in mine.

TEA = LIQUID WISDOM

"I'm sorry about the ring, Aldo," said Goosy. "How are you feeling about it?"

"Bad," I said.

"Bad how?" she asked.

"Bad that Jack thought it was real, but I didn't really listen to him." *Bad that I blew my chance to get a flat-screen TV.*

"Bad karma," she said, shaking her head.

There was that word again! Karma!

"Buddhists believe in karma. Karma means getting back what you give, spiritually speaking," said Goosy. "So if you treat other people with kindness and generosity, that's what you'll you get in return. But if you treat others badly..."

"You get badness back," I finished. "So the ring got lost because I was being mean to Jack?"

"Maybe." Goosy shrugged and slurped her tea.

"The ring got lost because I dropped it and it just flat-out disappeared," I said, frowning at her.

"Maybe it will reappear if you work on your karma," she said, leaning over to kiss me on the head. "Oops, we forgot to take off our hairnets."

On the drive home, I thought about what Goosy said. What goes around, comes around. I'd heard that before, but I didn't know what it meant. Now maybe I did.

(A KIND OF TEA THEY SHOULD MAKE.)

LATE-NIGHT TV

I'm supposed to be in bed, but I can't sleep, so I snuck downstairs to watch TV. Besides, bedtimes during summer vacation are totally bogus.

I keep thinking about where the ring could be! I'm going to look through all the kitchen drawers one more time...

OK, I checked the drawers again. No ring. Arg.

The Food Channel is one of my TV favorites. Right now there's this show on about Mardi Gras, which is the big parade and party they put on every February in New Orleans. They eat so much great food during Mardi Gras! Jambalaya (which is like a stew), Cajun shrimp, and this cake called King Cake. It's kind of like a sweet bread, and the person who makes it puts a dried red bean or a tiny plastic baby inside it. (I know, weird, but the cake itself looks delicious.) Whoever gets the hidden treasure in their piece of cake has good luck for the whole next year.

Hey! Did anyone check the <u>sugar</u> canister for the ring? I'm gonna go look.

Nope. Not there either.

Now the Mardi Gras show is over, and there's this long infomercial on about something called the Miracle Oven.

It's this awesome little baking appliance you put on your counter and you use it to make every yummy kind of food imaginable.

Moist chicken! Tender roasts! Pizza! Cookies!

I think there's a bag of peanut butter cookies in the cupboard. BRB.*

I'm back. We definitely need a Miracle Oven! I feel like I should wake up my mom and dad right now to tell them about it, because if we order within the next 10 minutes we get a special Miracle Oven cookbook absolutely free! Wait, there's more! If we order right now, we also get free super-duper baking mitts that my dad would love!

It cleans up easily and is so much healthier for you than regular oven-cooking and it's nonstick and deli cious

I must have fallen asleep because the next thing I knew, my mom was shaking my arm to wake me up. It was morning, and the TV was still blaring,* and the empty bag of peanut butter cookies was sitting on my chest.

I was busted.* And feeling a little bilious.*

"Go brush your teeth, Aldo," my mom said. "And take a shower and clean your room."

The abominable triple penalty.

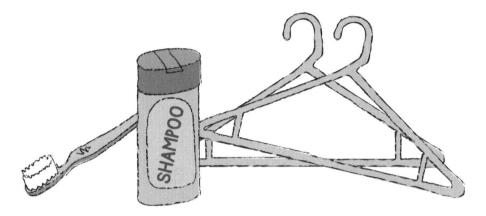

But I did all 3 things, and now I'm in my room with my betta fish. He looks pretty content there, hanging out with the Buddha.

When my mom woke me up, I remembered I'd had this bizarre* dream about my comic strip characters. The Miracle Oven foods had met up with Bacon Boy and Voracio. Guess I'd better write it down if I want to work on getting richer and famouser.

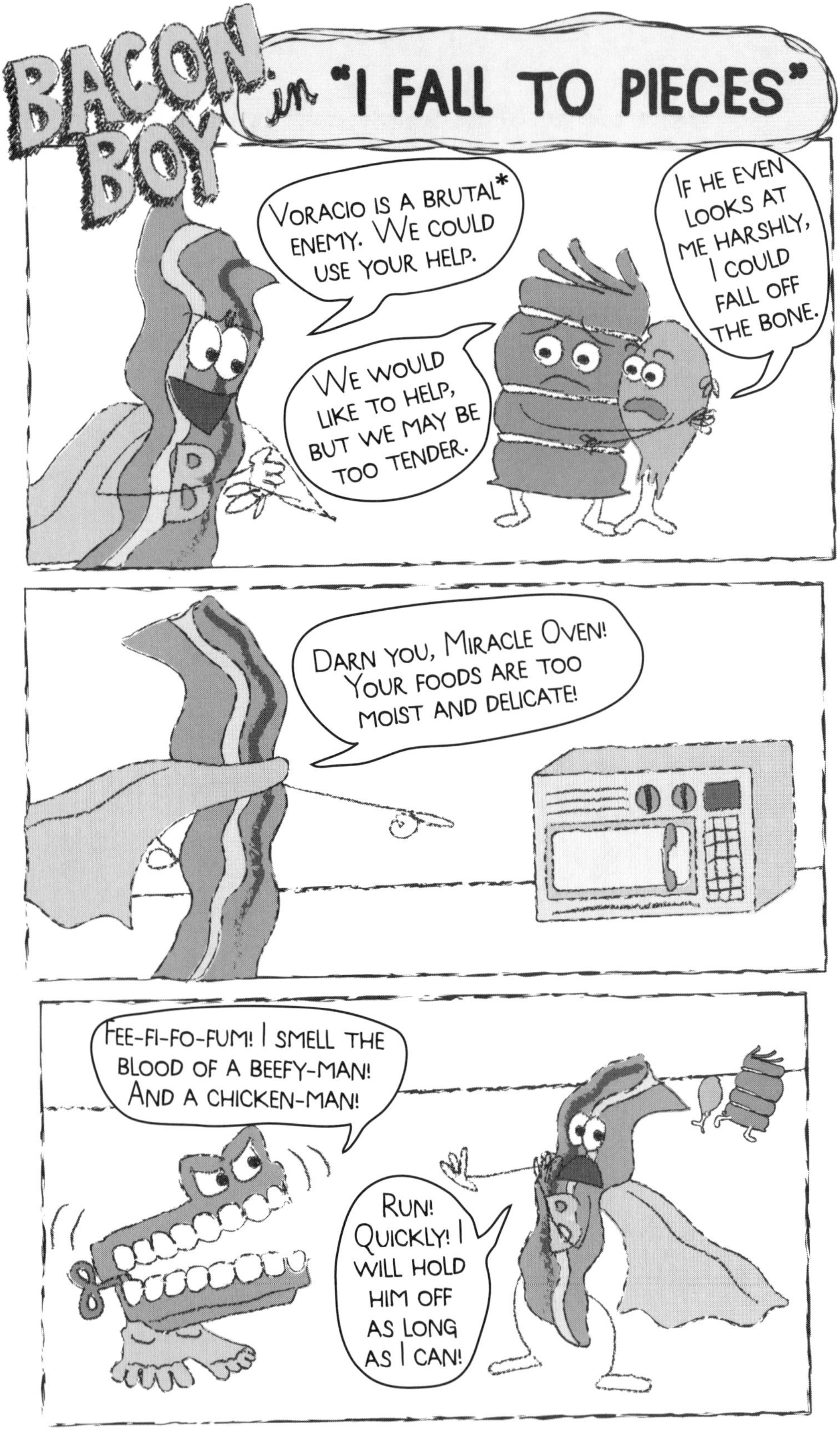

BACON BOY in "I FALL TO PIECES"
VORACIO IS A BRUTAL* ENEMY. WE COULD USE YOUR HELP.
WE WOULD LIKE TO HELP, BUT WE MAY BE TOO TENDER.
IF HE EVEN LOOKS AT ME HARSHLY, I COULD FALL OFF THE BONE.
DARN YOU, MIRACLE OVEN! YOUR FOODS ARE TOO MOIST AND DELICATE!
FEE-FI-FO-FUM! I SMELL THE BLOOD OF A BEEFY-MAN! AND A CHICKEN-MAN!
RUN! QUICKLY! I WILL HOLD HIM OFF AS LONG AS I CAN!

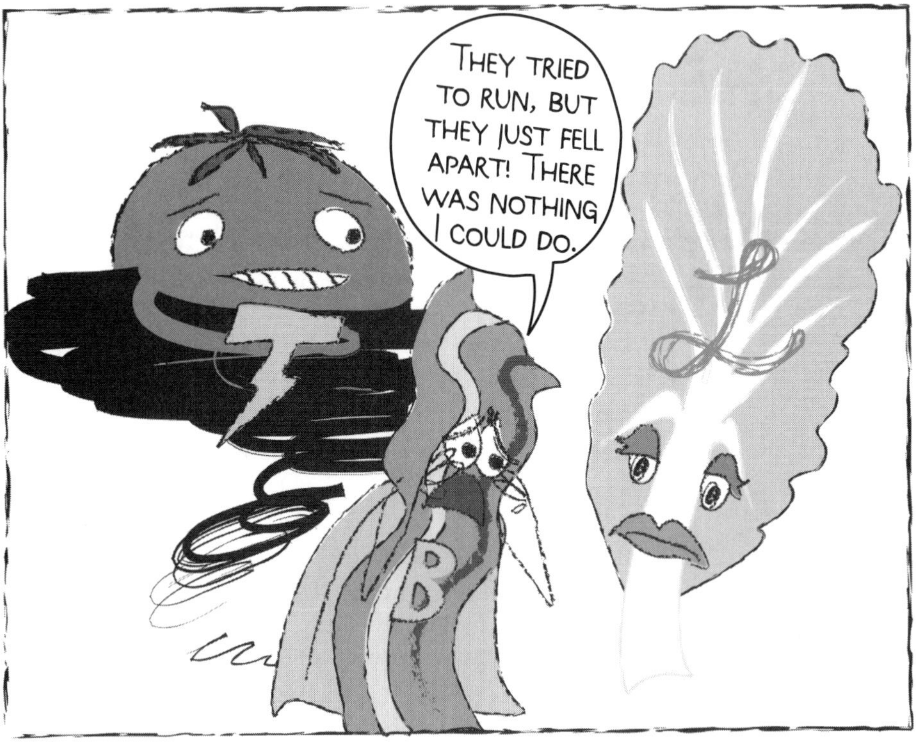
THEY TRIED TO RUN, BUT THEY JUST FELL APART! THERE WAS NOTHING I COULD DO.

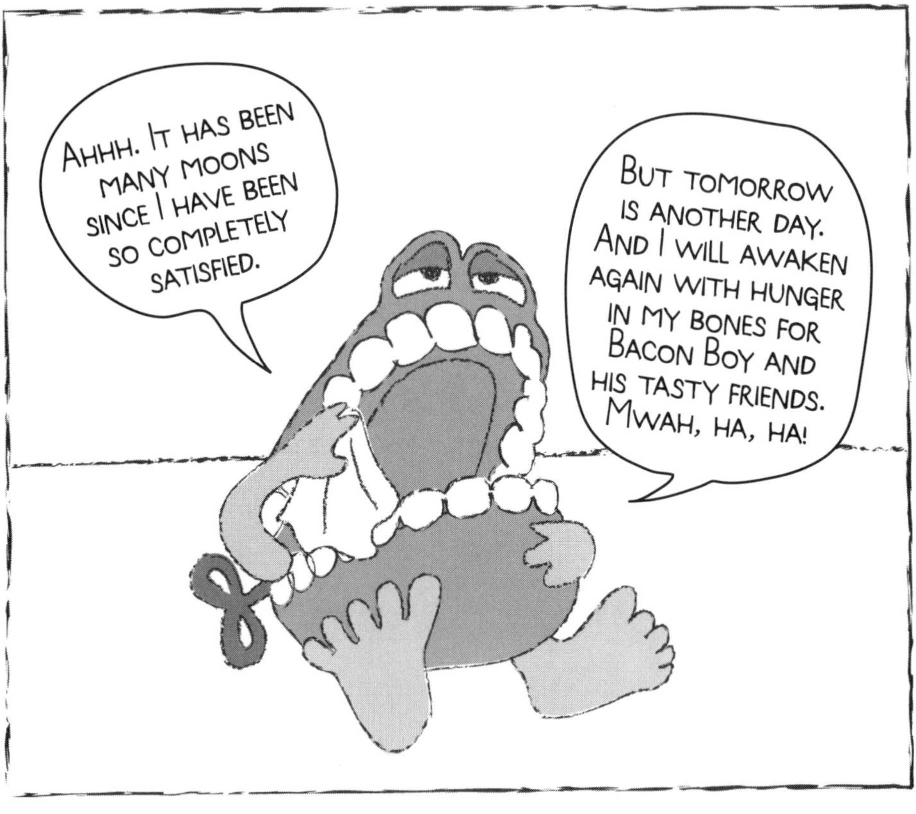
AHHH. IT HAS BEEN MANY MOONS SINCE I HAVE BEEN SO COMPLETELY SATISFIED.
BUT TOMORROW IS ANOTHER DAY. AND I WILL AWAKEN AGAIN WITH HUNGER IN MY BONES FOR BACON BOY AND HIS TASTY FRIENDS. MWAH, HA, HA!

THE GREAT STUPID

I'm in the car with Goosy, Timothy, Jack, Bee, and my mom on our way to some crazy place called The Great Stupid.

I know. I can't believe that there's actually a place called The Great Stupid either. But apparently there is.

So anyway, it's in the mountains about an hour from our house. Goosy called and said she wanted to take us there because it's something everyone should see. "And Aldo..." she said, whispering to me. "It's a place where you can clear your mind. Maybe the ring's destiny will come to you."

That would be good...

"Going to the mountains is a wonderful idea!" Mom said. "It's a beautiful day, and we can be OUTSIDE and get some FRESH AIR!"

Yippee.

I'll write about The Great Stupid after we check it out.

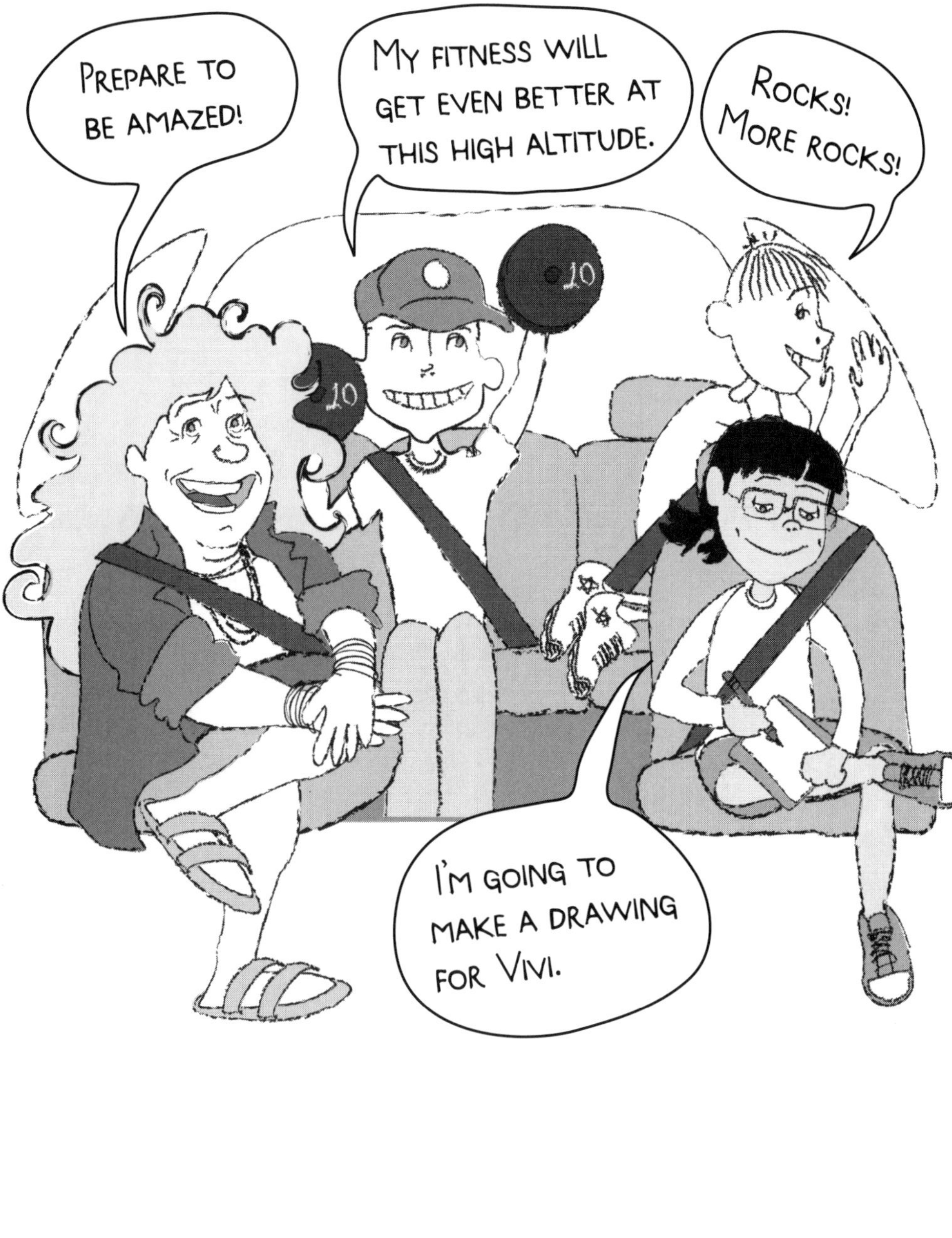
PREPARE TO BE AMAZED!
MY FITNESS WILL GET EVEN BETTER AT THIS HIGH ALTITUDE.
ROCKS! MORE ROCKS!
10
10
I'M GOING TO MAKE A DRAWING FOR VIVI.

OK, I'm back. First of all I need to register a complaint.

This Great Stupa (I found out that's what it's called...not the Great Stupid) IS a pretty cool place. But you have to walk—uphill—to get there! I did not agree to a hike. I fell down and scraped practically all the skin off my knee. Fortunately, Mom had a bandaid. (It was a bacon bandaid, which, if you need a bandaid, is the best kind because bacon always makes you feel better.)

When we FINALLY got there, I was pretty amazed, just like Goosy said. It's this uber-fancy Asian temple kind of deal, painted white but decorated with real gold and bright colors. It reminded me of one of the fancy wedding cakes my dad sometimes makes.

And inside is a giant statue of Buddha. Only this one doesn't look like the laughing Buddha I put in my betta fish's bowl. This one is skinny and has long, droopy ears.

The guide lady told us that's what the word
stupa means...a big Buddha statue. She had us
all sit criss-cross-applesauce on cushions on the
temple floor while she talked to us. She said that
stupas aren't like my church back home. They're not
for worshipping, and Buddha isn't a god. He was
just a regular guy who learned how to be perfectly
awesome. Then he taught other people how to try
to be perfectly awesome by meditating and thinking
only nice, peaceful thoughts.

"Stupas promote harmony, good health, and peace," she said.

I raised my hand. "What about good luck?"

"Actually, Buddhists believe there is no such think as luck," she said. "Instead, there is only how you choose to act. If you are a good and positive person, good and positive things will happen to you in return."

That sounded an awful lot like the karma thing Goosy was telling me about. Sigh. I could use some good old-fashioned <u>luck</u> about now.

Then the guide lady said we would close our visit to The Great Stupa with a short meditation. We were still sitting on our cushions, and she told us to think this thought: "I am a bearer of love and joy." But instead, I meditated on this idea: "I am a bearer of rings." And I thought about the time I was a ringbearer in my cousin's wedding. Maybe that will do the trick.

Before we left The Great Stupa, just in case, I climbed up and sneaked a <u>quick</u> rub of the Buddha statue's belly. Buddhists might not believe in good luck, but I'm gonna.

LET US EAT CAKE!

All the way home from The Great Stupa I had this tingly, super-aware feeling, like something important was about to happen.

So when we walked into the kitchen and I saw my dad decorating a giant beach cake, I had this sudden moment of <u>knowing</u>.

AND ONE LAST STARFISH... TA-DA!

I guess all that meditating really did clear my mind. I remembered it all super sharply, in slow motion...the ring on my right thumb, my hand swiping some cake batter out of the bowl, Max jumping over the counter, my left hand smooshing into the bowl of blueberries, my ringless right hand lifting out of the batter bowl...

The ring was in the cake, even though my dad had stirred the cake batter to check for the ring before he baked it. He must have missed it, that's all. And the cake, which had been frozen until it was time to frost and decorate it, was on the counter. Right here in front of us.

"I need that cake, Dad," I said.

"It's for the big neighborhood party on Saturday."

"But I need it right now."

"We have other things you can snack on, Aldo. How about a peanut butter sandwich?"

"You read my mind, Mr. Z," said Jack.

"Dad!" I was starting to get a little apoplectic. "That cake is worth $1,000!"

"Why thank you! It is a beauty, isn't it." He stuck the flag in the top then stepped back to admire his work.

"Dad. Jack. Everybody. Listen to me. The. Ring. Is. In. The. Cake."

And I explained my memory pictures and the TV show about the King Cake and how I just knew in my bones that the ring had been found.

Jack smiled. Bee smiled. Even my dad smiled. Then he said, "Well, guess we'll find out for sure on Saturday! If you're right, that'll add a little excitement to our neighborhood party."

What? "We have to get the ring out of the cake RIGHT NOW!"

"Sorry, Charlie. This cake is very special, and we're not cutting into it before the party."

I dropped to the floor and started kicking and screaming. Sometimes throwing a fit gets my dad to bargain.* But it didn't work this time.

"No way, José," Dad said. "If it's in the cake, we'll find it on Saturday. Until then, this beautiful behemoth* is going to chill out in the refrigerator in the garage."

Saturday is 2 days away. That is <u>forever</u>.

THINGS THAT ARE BOGUS

Here is my top-10 list of things that I think are bogus:

10. INFOMERCIALS

9. CANADIAN BACON
   (Who cares where it's from! It's not bacon!)

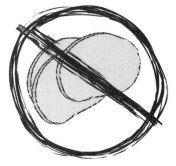

8. MAGIC TRICKS
   (Timothy!)

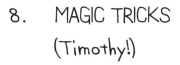

7. STUFF ON eBAY
(Did you know that
a piece of toast that
supposedly looked like
Albert Einstein sold for
$384? C'mon.)

6. BUDDHISM (I just found out
that some Buddhists
don't eat meat!
That's bonkers!*)

5. BEDTIMES during
summer vacation

4. VEGETABLES (Sorry,
Bee, but that's the
cold, hard truth.)

3.   OUTSIDE

2.   GIVING MONEY
to help people
you don't
even know

1.   MY DAD not letting
us look for the ring in
his stupid cake!

THE METAL DETECTOR

Today I awakened to Jack sticking some kind of a machine into my face.

"Aldo! Wake up! I know how we can tell for sure if the ring is in the cake!"

I rolled over and squinted at the clock. "Jack! It's barely 8." Even a giant flat-screen TV isn't important at 8 a.m. on a sleep-in summer morning. Geez Louise.

"We'll use my metal detector! All we have to do is wand it over the cake, and we'll be able to tell if there's something metal inside it!"

Jack was waving his metal detector over the top of my dresser, and it was making this hugely annoying beeping sound.

"There's metal somewhere on your dresser, Aldo."

"Geez, you think?" I said, rolling out of bed and stumbling over to my dresser. My poor fish was glaring at me. I think Jack woke him up too. I reached into the fishbowl and pulled out the dripping-wet laughing Buddha. "Here. Metal."

"Cool. Now let's detect the cake," said Jack.

"OK, OK."

So we crept downstairs and ever-so-quietly slipped into the garage. We opened the old refrigerator that my dad uses for storing big cakes. There it was...the giant beach cake that would make us rich and famous.

Jack poked the metal detector into the refrigerator, and it immediately started blaring.

"Can't you make it quieter?" I said. "My mom and dad are gonna hear us!"

"OK. I'll put on the earphones," said Jack. "But the problem with this old refrigerator is that the shelves are made of metal, and the detector is detecting the shelves. Let's take the cake out."

So I hoisted one side of the big pan holding the cake, and Jack hoisted the other side. It was so heavy... but somehow we didn't drop it. (You thought I was going to say we dropped it, didn't you?)

We set the pan on the garage floor, and Jack was just starting to move the metal detector over the top of the cake when Max came bounding* into the garage. We must have left the door into the garage ajar.

"Maxie, stop!" I said. He was hurtling straight toward the cake!

Jack wasn't paying any attention to Max. He was too focused on the metal detector, which was starting to blink near the cake's sailboat decoration.

So I dove onto Max and flattened him like one of our sidewalk pancakes.

The detector was blinking more insistently now, and Jack was smiling from earphone to earphone.

I heard a tap at the window behind me and turned to see Tommy Geller's oversized noggin. He had a great big smile plastered on his face too. He'd seen what we were doing!

And that's when my dad walked into the garage.

Needless to say, Jack and I didn't get to do any more cake detecting today. Dad whisked it back into the fridge and banished* me and Jack from the garage for the rest of our lives. But now we not only know the ring is in the cake, we've pinpointed that it's behind the sailboat. And we need to get that sailboat piece before Tommy does.

JUST THINK OF THE THINGS I'LL NEVER HAVE TO DO BECAUSE I'M NOT ALLOWED IN THE GARAGE! EXCELLENT.

GOOD LUCK

It's the morning of the neighborhood party! Today's the big day. Today we'll get our $1,000 reward and Jack will realize that <u>my</u> bedroom is a much better place for the flat-screen TV. I mean, the lighting in my room is perfect, and I have this big empty wall on one side. Jack doesn't really have the wall space for a flat-screen TV. His room is full of windows and rockshelves (that's what you have when your bookshelves are full of rocks instead of books...rockshelves).

I don't think I slept a wink last night. I kept thinking and thinking and thinking about the ring. And today I'm so excited I can barely be still...and believe me, I can ALWAYS be still. I am the king of being still. The phrase "being still" has my picture next to it in the dictionary.

OK, so now I'm getting the laughing Buddha out of the fishbowl and rubbing its wet, slimy belly for luck. Ew. (Somebody needs to clean that bowl.)

Still can't sit still. I'm going to meditate to calm myself down. BRB.

So I tried clearing my mind of everything __except__ an image of a giant flat-screen TV. A perfect, beautiful flat-screen TV floating on high. In my meditation, birds chirped and harp music played. Choirs of angels sang.

BE GENEROUS, ALDO!

But someone kept trying to enter my thoughts and push the TV aside. It was Goosy. I saw her face floating in the clouds with sun streaming behind it. "Karma means getting back what you give," she said, repeating what she'd told me at the tea factory that day. "If you treat other people with kindness and generosity, that's what you'll you get in return."

When I tried to shake the image of Goosy and reimagine the flat-screen TV, guess who appeared? Bacon Boy!

I KNOW, IT'S HARD BEING THE HERO. BUT SOMEBODY HAS TO DO IT.

OK, OK. For this <u>one day</u> I'm going to be kind and generous so that I'm sure to get back kindness and generosity. I'm taking all my Slushie money to Bee's house, and I'm putting it in her Bhutan jar. Right now. Karma, here I come.

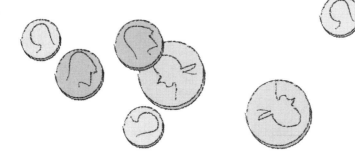

JUST DESSERTS

Every summer all the people in our neighborhood get together for a party at the neighborhood swimming pool.

There are swimming games for the kids and lots of lounging and blabbing for the grown-ups. Normally I love the swimming games. As you might expect, Jack and I rule at the game where the lifeguards toss cans of soda into the pool and kids dive to get them. Plus, I usually place pretty high in the belly-flop contest.

But this year Jack and I couldn't concentrate on the swimming games. All we could think about was the cake. But the cake-cutting wasn't going to happen until after lunch, even though we tried to get my dad to reconsider the blatantly* bogus rule of eating dessert AFTER the meal.

"Forget about it, boys," he said, shooing us away. "The cake cutting is at least 2 hours away. Go play."

"OK, but you have to PROMISE us that we'll get the sailboat piece."

"I promise."

I practically had to drag Jack away from that cake, because his precious ring was right there, so close, just waiting to be rescued. But I managed to persuade him that we should go to our fort, just for a few minutes, to relax and talk about what to do with the reward money.

So Jack and I walked over to the fort. Bee was already there, brushing her hair. (Oh geez. That was exactly what I was afraid of. Girliness—in our fort! But then she belched,* which made me feel OK again about her being in our club.)

BURP! Oooh, THAT FELT GOOD

"Thanks for donating your Slushie money this morning, Aldo," she said. "I know how much Slushies mean to you."

"You put money in the Bhutan jar?" said Jack. "Cool."

We sprawled on the fort ground and stared up into the branches of the pine tree. It was a hot, sunny day, and it felt good in the cool shade.

"So, uh, Jack..." I said. "What are we...uh, you...thinking about doing with the reward money?" I was playing it cool, trying to sound as if I didn't care in the least.

"I dunno," he said. "It's fun to think about all the different things you could buy with that much money. Like, we could get every video game we ever wanted."

"Yeah," I admitted. "I couldn't even sleep last night because I kept thinking about all the possibilities. Especially the possibility that's flat and has a big screen..."

"I've always wanted one of those humongous amethyst geodes they sell in the rock store downtown," he said.

Oh great. I knew that if Jack got to choose, he'd buy $1,000 worth of rocks.

"You could buy gifts for your families," suggested Bee. "That would be fun."

"Uh, no," I said brusquely.* "It wouldn't."

We kept talking for a bit longer, then something happened. It felt like that scene in *The Wizard of Oz* where Dorothy and Lion walk through the poppy field and suddenly get so tired that they have to lie down and sleep—even though they would be in the Emerald City in just a few more steps.

Somehow, Jack and Bee and I fell asleep! Except no snowfall or flying monkeys or munchkins woke us up. Eventually, Pong (one of Bee's cats) crawled into our fort and started meowing loudly, maybe because no one was home to feed him.

"Meow!" said Pong.

"Holy cow!" said Bee.

"Let's go, now!" said Jack.

And Bee and Jack took off running back to the swimming pool, with me following behind as closely as I could, considering I'm running-impaired.

When we got back to the party, it was obvious we'd missed the cake cutting. Everybody was shoveling cake into their mouths like it was the last pastry in the universe.

A group of grown-ups was standing around Dad, shaking his hand and telling him it was the best cake they'd ever eaten. He was grinning, and as I ran up to him and screamed, "Where's my piece of cake?", he chuckled and shook his head, as if to say to the other adults, *Kids, they love their cake!*

"Aldo, calm down," he said. "Your friend Tommy is bringing you your slice. He's a very considerate young man. There he is, at that picnic table."

I turned to see Tommy Geller holding his fork like you'd hold a ski pole. And he was stabbing it into a monstrous mound of Dad's blueberry beach cake.

That heart implosion feeling came over me again, but this time it gave me courage. I stepped toward Tommy, ready to use whatever tactics I had to—throwing a fit in public, faking the bubonic plague,* barfing on his head—to get the ring that was rightfully, well, <u>not</u> Tommy's. But before I could even choose which tactic to start with, Tommy said, "Here's your piece, Aldo." And he pointed at a second plate of cake next to him. One with a big frosting sailboat on its side.

I looked at Jack and Bee, who were just as blown away as I was, and I stuck my hand into the piece of cake Tommy had saved for me. Within a few seconds, I'd found it. My pinky finger felt something hard and very much uncakey. So I dug it out and bent down to swish it in the swimming pool, cleaning off the icing and crumbs so I could see it better. And there it was, shining in the July sun. Our bewitching,* brilliant, unbogus diamond ring.

I handed the ring to Jack for safekeeping, because I knew that if anyone would take good care of it, it would be Jack. Then Jack and Bee and I joined together in a happy dance that turned into a bunny hop. We were so boisterous* that lots of our neighbors turned to watch then began to join in. Pretty soon the whole party was bunny-hopping around the pool.

Eventually we gathered up my parents and Goosy and Mr. Mot and Timothy and Jack's parents—both sets—and Bee's family and showed the ring to all of them and told and retold the whole story. Tommy Geller listened and smiled, and my dad patted him on the back. (I know! Uber-weird!)

Mom had saved the phone number of the ring's owner from the newspaper article, and we called her. She wasn't home, so we had to leave a message, but I'd bet anything that tomorrow we'll have our reward.

I KNEW TOMMY GELLER WOULD TURN OUT TO BE A GOOD GUY.

Jack still has the ring. I'm glad he gets to keep it in his room for one night.

You know how some days are so crazy and hectic and awesome that when you come home and you lie down in your bedroom and watch your betta fish, the world suddenly seems so quiet? And because of that quiet, you're able to remember the day, and your remembering of the day is almost as good as—maybe even better than—the living of the day was?

That's right now.

FORTUNE AND GLORY

This morning Jack and Bee came to my house bright and early because the lady who owns the ring called to say she was on her way over. The lady also called the newspaper, so when our doorbell rang and Jack and I answered it, there was the lady AND a reporter AND a photographer.

The night before, Jack had given the ring another bath then rubbed it with some special gemstone polish, so even I had to admit that it looked amazing. I don't know how anyone ever thought this obviously special ring was bogus. Sheesh.

The lady was so happy to see it that she cried and hugged each one of us. Her husband had given her the ring a long time ago, but he was gone now. (She didn't say where he went, though. Brazil? Barcelona? Brindisi? Who knows.)

Then came the part I'd been dreaming about for days and days. The lady took out her checkbook and asked whom she should make the $1,000 reward check payable to. I looked at Jack and kept my mouth shut. *My karma worked yesterday,* I was thinking. *Maybe if I'm kind and generous to Jack this morning, he'll karma me right back with at least a smallish flat-screen.*

Jack stepped forward. "I don't really need $1,000," he said. (My heart imploded again.) "But I know someone who does. Bee, what's the name of your pen-pal in Bhutan?"

"This is just what I wished for!" said Bee.

This isn't happening, I thought. I pinched my leg to wake myself up. "Ouuuch!" I said. Everyone turned to look at me.

But Bee buzzed home and brought back her Bhutan jar anyway. The lady wrote the reward check, and the photographer snapped a picture of me and Jack and Bee and the Bhutan jar and the ring and the lady sticking the check into the top of the jar.

This was followed by lots of congratulating hugs and comments from the grown-ups like "We're so proud of you kids" and "Who says the younger generation is selfish?"

Blah, blah, blah.*

THE PICTURE THAT WAS IN THE NEWSPAPER THE NEXT DAY

Later, after everyone had gone home, I went up to my room. I sat in my beanbag chair and stared at the big, blank wall where the flat-screen TV wasn't.

Timothy walked in, balancing a pencil on his nose.

"What'd you name your betta fish?" he asked.

"Nothing."

"Do you wanna play catch?"

"No."

"You don't really think you need a flat-screen TV more than that girl needs food, do you, bro?"

I sighed and slid to the floor. "Well can we at least go get a Slushie?"

"I guess."

"Can you pay? Because I put all my money in that stupid jar yesterday."

"If you do my chore today. Folding laundry."

My reward: More lint. Sigh.

SWEET REWARD

Here was the headline in this morning's newspaper:

The article told the whole ring story, from beginning to end. Jack and Bee and I are famous now! Welp, I said I wanted to get richer and famouser, right? Famouser, check. Richer, not so much.

After Mr. Mot saw the article, he came to my house to congratulate me.

"Well done, Aldo!" he said. "I'm proud to know you and your friends. Did you realize that Charles Schulz was a philanthropist too?"

"Who's Charles Schulz?" I was playing a video game, and I was kinda distracted.

"The famous cartoonist I was telling you about. The one who created the Peanuts comics."

"Oh yeah. He was a paleontologist?" We learned about paleontology in school last year. It's when you study fossils. I pictured the guy with a cartooning pen in one hand and a dinosaur bone in the other. Weird.

"No, a philanthropist. That means he donated his own money—millions and millions of dollars in his case—to causes he thought would help other people, such as libraries. Actually, he spent very little money on himself."

"So he made millions from his comic strips? Cool."

"That's not the point, Aldo."

"Yeah, I know. But still."

Later Jack and Bee and I met at the fort.
I brought my betta fish along because he seemed
bored. It was a boring afternoon, but it was the
kind of boring that's nice once in a while.

"I wrote a letter to my pen-pal and told her
we'd be sending $1,000 to her school," said Bee.
"They'll use the money to buy more nourishing food
for the kids."

"Like hot dogs?" I asked.

"I'm not sure. Maybe tofu."

"What?" Our jar of beautiful money will be wasted on soybean curd?

"Most of the families in my pen-pal's village are Buddhist, Aldo. Lots of them are vegetarian. And they love super-spicy chilies."

"Cool," said Jack. He was still smiling. I don't think he'd stopped smiling ever since we got the ring back.

Just then the branches at the side of the fort rustled, and Goosy's head popped through. "Can I come in?"

No grown-up had ever been in our fort before, but Goosy's barely a grown-up. So we said OK. She crawled in on her hands and knees and sat on the ground beside us.

"I adore it in here!" she said. "It's so shadowy and cozy. I should make a painting of it sometime."

Goosy had brought a bulging* white paper bag with her. Inside were doughnuts...yummy, gigantic doughnuts of all kinds. Chocolate-covered, raspberry-filled, rainbow-sprinkled, double-glazed.

"Everybody deserves a reward now and then, just for being the bodacious* people we all are," she said, and she let us each pick 2.

I fed some doughnut crumbs to my betta, who seemed to be enjoying his field trip.

"I decided what to name my fish," I said. "I'm gonna call him Bogus."

"¡Bueno!" said Jack. Bee giggled.

"I adore it!" said Goosy. "And I adore all of you. Now let's go play badminton.*"

So we did. B4N.*

"B" GALLERY

Mr. Mot used to be an English teacher. He's a word nerd, and he likes to help me use awesome words in my sketchbooks. I mark the best words with one of these: * (it's called an asterisk). When you see an * you'll know you can look here, in the Gallery, to see what the word means. If you don't know how to say some of the words, just ask Mr. Mot. Or someone you know who's like Mr. Mot. Or go to aldozelnick.com, and we'll say them for you.

B4N (pg. 140): bye for now

baby barf (pg. 54): when you throw up just a tiny amount in your mouth

baby fat (pg. 55): the kind of fat that cute, chubby babies and toddlers have (and even some 10-year-olds)

badminton (pg. 140): a sport (blech) you play with rackets, a tall net in the middle, and a kinda cool ball-thingy called a birdie

bailiwick (pg. 44): something that's your "thing," something you really like

baller (pg. 36): somebody who's good at sports (and likes to show off)

ballistic (pg. 17): crazy upset

banal (pg. 30): boring because it's the same every day

banished (pg. 119): sent away from somewhere and told you can't ever go back

bargain (pg. 110): make a deal, compromise

barged (pg. 74): pushed your way right on in

bazillion (pg. 82): lots, way more than you could count

bearded dragon (pg. 26): a kind of lizard people keep as pets. Has a ruffle of skin under the chin that looks like a beard—not an actual beard.

beaucoup (pg. 34): Frenchy word that means lots and lots

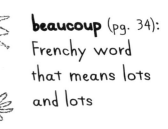

WHAM!

JUST COME ON IN, TOMMY!

beckoned (pg. 39): told you to come along without using words, just a hand wave or a head nod

bedlam (pg. 66): when all kinds of crazy, loud things are going on in a room all at once

beeline (pg. 62): when you're in a hurry to get somewhere so you take a straight and speedy path

behavior (pg. 83): how you act and what you do

behemoth (pg. 111): something that's supersized

belched (pg. 124): burped

bereft (pg. 90): sad because you lost something you cared about

berserk (pg. 45): crazy, wild upset

bespectacled (pg. 9): wears glasses

betta fish (pg. 27): a kind of freshwater fish that comes from Thailand and likes to fight with other fish, so they have to live by themselves in little bowls. I have one. I wonder if he likes Thai food?

bewildering (pg. 73): surprisingly weird and hard to understand

bewitching (pg. 129): magically attractive

Bhutan (pg. 40): this little country between India and China where Bee's pen-pal lives

bien (pg. 70): Spanish. *Oh bien* means Oh well.

bilingual (pg. 20): can speak two languages. I speak English and Slushie.

bilious (pg. 99): gross and grouchy

bitter (pg. 40): one of the five main kinds of tastes (the others are sweet, salty, sour, and savory). Bitter is pretty much the only nasty one if you ask me.

JUST THE PEEL.

THINGS THAT TASTE BITTER.

bizarre (pg. 99): really weird and strange

blabbermouth (pg. 78): someone who talks and talks and talks—and sometimes says things he's not supposed to

blah (pg. 29): bored and kind of sad

blah, blah, blah (pg. 134): when people (usually grown-ups) say boring or dumb stuff

blaring (pg. 98): LOUD! Like a car horn.

blast! (pg. 73): Darn! Dag nab it!

blatantly (pg. 123): obviously. So obviously that everyone knows it.

bleepity-bleep (pg. 75): a phrase that you use in place of what the person really said, because what the person really said is not appropriate for children and moms to hear

blip (pg. 47): an eensy bit

blithely (pg. 42): happily, cheerfully. Bee does everything blithely, I've noticed. It's annoying.

block, cartoonist's (pg. 22): when you're trying to be a good cartoon-maker, like Charles Schulz, but you're frustrated because you can't think of anything to draw

blockhead (pg. 11): a dumb person, a knucklehead

bloke (pg. 92): a British word for guy

bludgeon (pg. 138): smash with a club. Ouch.

blue (pg. 92): You looked up the word "blue"? It's a color! Hello! Oh, and it can also mean sad.

boa (pg. 26): a kind of snake that kills the animals it wants to eat by squeezing them to death. Isn't <u>that</u> nice.

bodacious (pg. 140): super, mega, uber awesome

bogus (pg. 11 and a lot of places in this sketchbook): Fake. Kinda also means something that you think is wrong even though other people might think it's right.

bohemian (pg. 8): somebody who loves life and having fun

boisterous (pg. 129): loud and wild

bok choy (pg. 39): some gross kind of Asian cabbage

bolted (pg. 63): took off really quickly

BOLTING TO THE HARDWARE STORE TO GET SOME BOLTS

bon voyage (pg. 7): French for goodbye and have a good trip (Hey, am I going somewhere?)

bona fide (pg. 7): real, genuine, not an imposter

bonkers (pg. 113): crazy crazy

botched (pg. 11): same as bungled

bouffant (pg. 28): a girl hairstyle with a big pile of hair on the top of the head. That is just wrong in so many ways.

bouldering (pg. 14): a sport where you climb around on big rocks. Uh, yeaaah.

bounding (pg. 117): running and jumping at the same time

bowl, singing (pg. 82): a copper bowl that sounds kinda like a bell when you rub its top edge

brain freeze (pg. 59): that icicle-in-the-head pain you get when you drink something uber-cold really fast. Also called ice cream headache.

brainstormed (pg. 86): thought up a ton of ideas, even if some of them are dumb

brazen (pg. 63): does brave stuff without worrying about it

BRB (pg. 97): be right back

breakdancing (pg. 71): a kind of dancing that is way too athletic and tiring

bric-a-brac (pg. 29): dumb little decorations you have on the shelves in your house

broiling (pg. 54): hot, hot, hot. So hot that it's the setting you use on your oven when you cook steaks.

brouhaha (pg. 76): a time when everybody's acting all loud and crazy

brusquely (pg. 126): short and abrupt (a tiny bit mean too)

brutal (pg. 100): harsh and kinda mean

bubonic plague (pg. 128): a terrible sickness that makes you look and feel like you're gonna die, cuz you probably are

Buddha (pg. 82): an Indian guy who lived thousands of years ago and was good at meditating

bueno (pg. 140): Spanish for *that's good*

bulging (pg 139): so full it's almost ready to burst

bummed (pg. 68): sad

bungled (pg. 11): messed up, ruined

busted (pg. 99): caught and in trouble

148

butler (pg. 26): a guy who's like your personal slave and does everything for you that you don't want to do

butter brickle (pg. 82): a kind of ice cream with yummy, hard bits of toffee mixed in

buzzkill (pg. 82): something or somebody that makes you sad right when you're in the middle of being happy

MY NEIGHBORHOOD

BASEBALL FIELD

TO THE GREAT STUPA

BEE'S HOUSE

BEE'S GARDEN

BEE'S CLIMBING TREE

MY HOUSE

MR.

SWIMMING POOL

GOOSY'S HOUSE

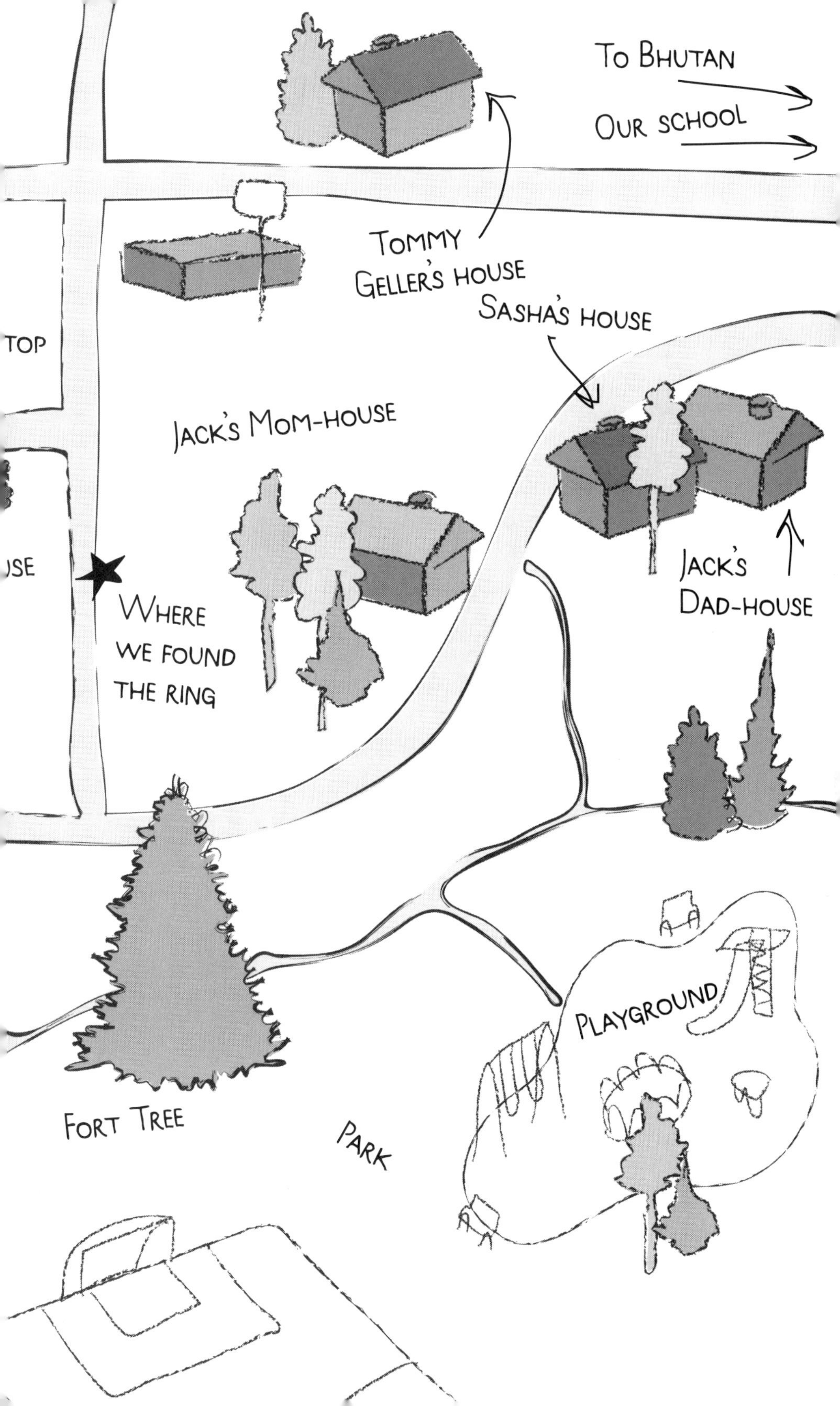

To Bhutan
Our school
Tommy
Geller's house
Sasha's house
TOP
Jack's Mom-house
USE
Where
we found
the ring
Jack's
Dad-house
Playground
Fort Tree
Park

ABOUT THE ALDO ZELNICK
COMIC NOVEL SERIES

The Aldo Zelnick comic novels are an alphabetical series for middle-grade readers aged 7-13. Rabid and reluctant readers alike enjoy the intelligent humor and drawings as well as the action-packed stories. They've been called vitamin-fortified *Wimpy Kids*.

Part comic romps, part mysteries, and part sesquipedalian-fests (ask Mr. Mot), they're beloved by parents, teachers, and librarians as much as kids.

ALSO IN THE ALDO ZELNICK COMIC NOVEL SERIES

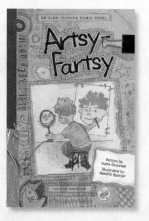

PUBLISHED DECEMBER 2009

Ten-year-old Aldo Zelnick isn't athletic like his brother, he's not a rock hound like his best friend, but he does like bacon.

And when his artist grandmother gives him a sketchbook to "record all his artsy-fartsy ideas," it turns out Aldo is a pretty good cartoonist.

But wait! Just when Aldo has decided he sorta *likes* drawing in his sketchook and leaves it in his fort overnight, a mystery girl comes along and draws flowers in it. Flowers! Aldo and Jack decide to figure out who she is, which leads to paying attention to girls and other appalling encounters.

In addition to an engaging cartoon story, *Artsy-Fartsy* includes an illustrated glossary of fun A words used throughout the book, such as *absurd*, *abominable*, and *audacious*.

For readers 7-13 | 160 pages | Hardcover
ISBN 978-1-934649-04-6 | $12.95

PUBLISHED MAY 2011

Summer is drawing to a close, and the Zelnicks travel to the family farm in Minnesota for their vacation. Aldo's mom is eager for him to experience the things she loved as a girl…shucking sweet corn, milking cows, gathering eggs. A week of FRESH AIR and living off the land!

But Aldo suspects that farm life isn't all it's cracked up to be…and it's worse than he feared. The rooster wakes him at dawn, the chores nearly do him in, and Timothy and the cousins—identical twin pranksters—are in cahoots against him. Plus, the creepy, old portrait of his great-grandfather Aldo (the very one he's named after) seems to be watching him from his frame on the wall…

All this without the comforts of TV or computer—because the Anderson farm is (gasp!) technology-free.

For readers 7-13 | 160 pages | Hardcover
ISBN 978-1-934649-08-4 | $12.95

BAILIWICK PRESS

309 East Mulberry Street | Fort Collins, Colorado 80524 | (970) 672-4878
www.bailiwickpress.com | www.aldozelnick.com

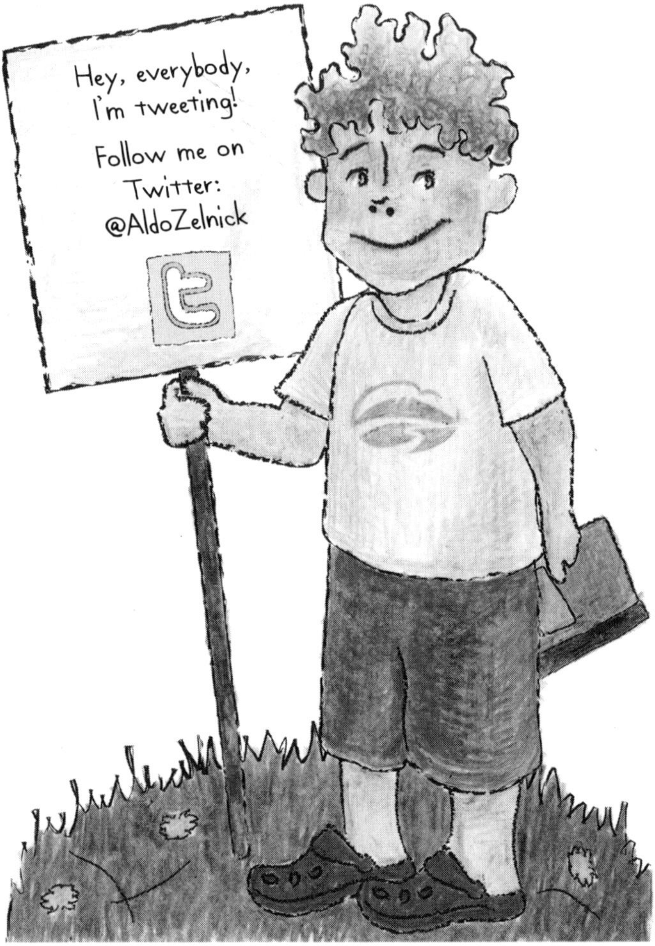
Hey, everybody,
I'm tweeting!
Follow me on
Twitter:
@AldoZelnick

VISIT ALDOZELNICK.COM TO...

- learn more about the next book in the series.
- hear how to pronounce the Gallery words.
- see the characters in full color.
- download coloring pages.
- suggest a word for an upcoming book.
- see Karla and Kendra's appearance schedule
  or invite them to your school, bookstore, or event.
- sign up for our e-mail list.

ACKNOWLEDGMENTS

"When you carry out acts of kindness, you get a wonderful feeling inside. It is as though something inside your body responds and says, yes, this is how I ought to feel."

- Harold Kushner

What an astonishing five months we've had since the publication of *Artsy-Fartsy*. It's scary sending a poor, defenseless little book out there into the world all by its lonesome. Will it find a place to live? Will it make friends?

We're thrilled that *Artsy-Fartsy* has indeed made friends—oodles of them. Kids, parents, teachers, librarians—everyone seems genuinely smitten with Aldo and his alphabetical adventures. A profound thank you to all who sent kudos for *Artsy-Fartsy*. Your comments and cheerleading made us believe we really could—and should—finish *Bogus* and fondly shove it out the door to keep its A sibling company.

Thanks also to our families, for your unstinting support; the Slow Sanders, for your always-essential critiques; Jean and Ava, for your eagle-eye editing; Launie, for your inimitable design; and Amy-the-audacious-intern, for your work launching *Artsy-Fartsy* into the blogosphere, proofing and reproofing *Bogus*, and generally being a help when we needed it most.

Speaking of being a help, poor Aldo. In *Bogus* he's forced to consider the true bounty of selflessness. He would do well to learn from his Angels, whose acts of kindness continue to amaze. You're bodacious people with good karma in spades, and we thank you.

Barbara Anderson

Carol & Wes Baker

Butch Byram

Annie Dahlquist

Leigh Waller Fitschen

Teresa Funke

Sawyer Gray (and Chris and Sarah)

Griff Griffin

Calvin Halvorson & Bennett Zent (and Chet)

Dick & Peggy Hohm

Chris Hutchinson

IBPAB (Jana Knezovich, Linda Mahan, Paola Price, Starr Teague & Jacki Witlen)

Becky Jensen and Jake & Dane Johnson

Anne Keasling

Vicki & Bill Krug

Tutu, Cole & Grant Ludwin

Virginia MacKinnon

The Mouton-Hoeven Family

Jackie O'Hara & Erin Rogers

Betty Oceanak

David Orphanides

Jackie Peterson

Ryan Petros

Terri Lynn Berryman Rosen

John Schiller & Suzanne Holm

Virginia Shelton

Slow Sand Writers Society

Barb & Steve Spanjer

Dana Spanjer

Vince & Adrianne Tranchitella

Laura White Welciek

Ken, Hagen & Smithey Hashagen Wilson

HALO THERE!

If you're an Aldo Zelnick fan, e-mail info@bailiwickpress.com
and ask for details about becoming an Aldo's Angel.
Angels receive special opportunities such as pre-publication
discounts, free shipping, signed and personally
inscribed copies, naming rights, and listing in the
acknowledgments (especially fun for kids).

ABOUT THE AUTHOR

Karla Oceanak has been a voracious reader her whole life and a writer and editor for more than twenty years. In her career as a marketeer, Karla has written everything you can imagine, from brochures and packaging copy to ads, video scripts, and feature articles. She has also ghostwritten numerous self-help books. She lives with her husband, Scott, and their three boys in a house strewn with Legos, hockey gear, Pokémon cards, video games, books, and dirty socks in Fort Collins, Colorado. This is her second novel.

ABOUT THE ILLUSTRATOR

Kendra Spanjer divides her time between being "a writer who illustrates" and "an illustrator who writes"— an ambitious amalgam, indeed. She decided to cultivate her artistic side after discovering that the best part of chemistry class was entertaining her peers (and her professor) with "The Daily Chem Book" comic. Since then, her diverse body of work has appeared in a number of group and solo art shows, book covers, marketing materials, fundraising events, and public places. When she invents spare time for herself to fill, Kendra enjoys skiing, cycling, exploring, discovering new music, watching trains go by, decorating cakes with her sister, and making faces in the mirror.